The Bala Lake Killings

Simon McCleave is a multi-million copy bestselling author. Before writing crime novels, he worked in television and film. He was a Script Editor at the BBC, a producer at Channel 4 and a Story Analyst in Los Angeles. He worked on films such as *The Full Monty* and television series such as the BBC Crime Drama *Between The Lines*. As a script writer he wrote on series such as *Silent Witness*, *Murder In Suburbia*, *Teachers*, *Attachments*, *The Bill*, *Eastenders* and many more.

Also by Simon McCleave

DI Ruth Hunter

The Snowdonia Killings
The Harlech Beach Killings
The Dee Valley Killings
The Devil's Cliffs Killings
The Berwyn River Killings
The White Forest Killings
The Solace Farm Killings
The Menai Bridge Killings
The Conway Harbour Killings
The River Seine Killings
The Lake Vyrnwy Killings
The Chirk Castle Killings
The Portmeirion Killings
The Llandudno Pier Killings
The Denbigh Asylum Killings
The Wrexham Killings
The Colwyn Bay Killings
The Chester Killings
The Llangollen Killings
The Wirral Killings
The Abersoch Killings
The Bala Lake Killings

The DC Ruth Hunter Murder Case Series

Diary of a War Crime
The Razor Gang Murder
An Imitation of Darkness
This is London, SE15

The Anglesey Series – DI Laura Hart

The Dark Tide
In Too Deep
Blood on the Shore
The Drowning Isle
Dead in the Water

Psychological Thrillers

Last Night at Villa Lucia
Five Days in Provence (June 2025)

Simon McCleave

THE BALA LAKE KILLINGS

CANELO CRIME

First published in the United Kingdom in 2025 by Stamford Publishing Ltd

This edition published in the United Kingdom in 2025 by

Canelo Crime, an imprint of
Canelo Digital Publishing Limited,
20 Vauxhall Bridge Road,
London SW1V 2SA
United Kingdom

A Penguin Random House Company
The authorised representative in the EEA is Dorling Kindersley Verlag GmbH. Arnulfstr. 124, 80636 Munich, Germany

Copyright © Simon McCleave 2025

The moral right of Simon McCleave to be identified as the creator of this work has been asserted in accordance with the Copyright, Designs and Patents Act, 1988.

All rights reserved. No part of this publication may be reproduced or transmitted in any form or by any means, electronic or mechanical, including photocopy, recording, or any information storage and retrieval system, without permission in writing from the publisher.

No part of this book may be used or reproduced in any manner for the purpose of training artificial intelligence technologies or systems. In accordance with Article 4(3) of the DSM Directive 2019/790, Canelo expressly reserves this work from the text and data mining exception.

A CIP catalogue record for this book is available from the British Library.

Print ISBN 978 1 83598 283 9
ISBN 9781835982839

This book is a work of fiction. Names, characters, businesses, organizations, places and events are either the product of the author's imagination or are used fictitiously. Any resemblance to actual persons, living or dead, events or locales is entirely coincidental.

Cover design by Tom Sanderson

Cover images © Shutterstock

Printed and bound in Great Britain by Clays Ltd, Elcograf S.p.A.

Look for more great books at
www.canelo.co | www.dk.com

PROLOGUE

Bangor, North Wales

October 2021

Ashwin Choudary raised his hand with a modest wave as his constituents applauded. The warm, bustling sound of applause reverberated through the small but lively venue, Penrhyn Hall, mixing with the scent of salty air that clung to the coastal breeze. He'd been an MP representing this area for seven years now, and each time he spoke, it filled him with a deep sense of pride. Bangor, the oldest city in Wales, had a unique charm to it. Nestled along the coast of North Wales, its streets whispered tales of history – stories of monasteries that once stood where the cathedral now rose majestically. Across the water lay the Isle of Anglesey, visible through the haze, its rocky shore framed by the Britannia and Menai Suspension bridges.

Bangor itself was a place steeped in history, dating back to the 6th century. The city's name came from an old Welsh word for *a wattled enclosure*, a fitting metaphor for the way the city had developed into a vibrant, multicultural community. With 15 per cent of the city's population identifying as ethnic minorities – Asian, Arabic, Black and Mixed Race – Bangor had one of the highest rates of ethnicity in Wales. Yet, this diversity, as Ashwin knew all too well, also brought challenges. Recently, racial tensions had begun to bubble to the surface, with racist graffiti appearing on the sides of buildings and assaults driven by racial bigotry on the rise. But the real danger came from the extremist groups that had begun to make their presence known. Far-right movements like British Action had issued threats, and Ashwin had been at the centre of their hateful rhetoric.

As he made his way to the podium, Ashwin's heart skipped a beat, but he quickly steadied himself, drawing strength from the applause.

He gazed out at the crowd, his eyes tracing the diversity that filled the room. There was a mix of faces – some familiar, some new – but all united by a shared vision. He was here to open the Bangor Festival of Words.

'Thank you,' he said quietly into the microphone, his voice steady but filled with emotion. 'Thank you. I hope you know how happy I am to represent a constituency with such wonderful diversity and creative talent. This area, with its deep Welsh roots, history and tradition, has shaped me in ways I never imagined when I first arrived. Home to one of the largest slate mines in the world, docks that were once the lifeblood of shipbuilding, and a university that dates back to 1885. It draws students from all corners of the world, enriching our community and our lives.'

He paused, scanning the faces before him. His words seemed to hang in the air, settling into the hearts of many in the crowd.

'And,' he continued, his voice becoming more deliberate, 'the constituency has been deeply enhanced by immigration and…'

A sudden burst of boos erupted from the back of the room. The unexpected outburst caught Ashwin off guard. He turned, his eyes narrowing as he caught sight of two men. Members of a far-right group, judging by their appearance, postures and sneers. They were making loud, derisive gestures, trying to drown him out.

Before Ashwin could respond, the men stood up, their faces twisted with hatred. They began performing Nazi salutes. The crowd's mood shifted as the men's chants of 'Seig Heil, Seig Heil' echoed across the hall. The air thickened with tension.

Ashwin felt a chill settle in his chest, but he maintained his composure, knowing the police officers stationed around the room would quickly handle the situation.

'…it is a diversity that we should all celebrate,' Ashwin said, his voice unwavering, though the hostility in the room was palpable.

Chaos erupted as the police surged towards the men, attempting to escort them out. Shouts filled the air, and a scuffle broke out. A woman's scream pierced through the noise, and in an instant, the peaceful gathering had descended into turmoil.

'I'm so terribly sorry that we've been disrupted like this,' Ashwin murmured into the microphone, his voice strained, trying to calm the crowd.

But before he could continue, one of the men lunged at a police officer, knocking him to the ground with a vicious blow.

The man then pulled out a handgun and pushed his way towards the stage, his eyes burning with anger and rage. His cropped blond hair and tattoos – a swastika and a Union Jack on his arms – were unmistakeable signs of his violent, twisted ideology.

'Choudary, you scum,' he hissed, the words dripping with venom as he barrelled forward, pushing people out of his way.

Ashwin's pulse quickened. His mind raced, trying to process the situation. He was in real danger. His legs trembled beneath him, and his heart hammered in his chest. Was this really happening? Was this the moment he was going to die?

The man was closing in, his eyes wild with hatred.

Daniel Orme, a local Labour councillor, tried to step in, but was quickly knocked aside. The man climbed onto the stage, eyes fixed on Ashwin, as if he were prey.

The gunman's voice rang out, his words filled with conviction. 'This is a strike for Britain!'

Ashwin's blood ran cold.

Then, there was a sharp, deafening CRACK – a gunshot.

The world around Ashwin seemed to freeze.

For a moment, he felt nothing, only a numbing shock, as if his body was suspended in time. Then, a searing, white-hot pain shot through his chest. He gasped, clutching his side. Blood began to soak into his shirt.

Another CRACK rang out, this time hitting him in the shoulder and sending him sprawling backwards, his body slamming against the floor.

The room swam in and out of focus.

His head was heavy, his breathing shallow.

He heard shouting – yelling – but it all felt distant. The pain in his chest was unbearable, and his thoughts grew foggy. The sound of rushing footsteps, the harsh grip of hands pulling him aside – all of it faded as his mind drifted away.

The world tilted as Ashwin lost his grip on consciousness.

As darkness took him, the last thing he saw was the glow of the ceiling lights, their soft vanilla hue casting an ethereal glow on the chaos below.

CHAPTER 1

Detective Inspector Ruth Hunter turned off the ignition of her car, her eyes momentarily lingering on the view before her. She had just pulled into her space at Llancastell Police Station. Well, it wasn't technically 'her space'. But it was where she parked every day, and anyone who dared to take it would hear about it, regardless of rank or title. The small ritual of parking, the routine of it all, grounded her. There was something comforting about predictability, especially in a life that seemed, more often than not, to be filled with uncertainty and chaos. She supposed that most people did crave routine. It freed the mind to focus on more important things. Where to park, which way to walk up to CID, the humdrum of others' chatter. Those were decisions that didn't require thought.

Ruth's mind drifted, as it often did, to her time in London. She remembered when she'd been seconded up to Scotland Yard, the gruelling four-month period spent travelling from Balham to Victoria every morning. The rhythm of her commute had become second nature. She stood in the same spot on the platform, entered through the same doors of the same tube carriage, and always took the same seat. The monotony had brought its own kind of peace. Routine was a comfort, a way to escape the noise of London's rush hour.

Ruth then glanced at her watch, noting the time. The craving for a cigarette surged again, stronger than ever. Despite her best efforts to quit, despite Daniel's pleading and Sarah's concern, it remained a constant companion. Ruth had tried everything: patches, gum, even hypnotherapy, but nothing worked. Deep down, she knew why. She just loved it. There was no other way to explain it. The slow burn, the rush, the long deep drag of smoke. No matter how much harm it caused, it was a part of her.

Pulling out a cigarette, she smiled to herself as she lit it, inhaling deeply. The smoke curled in the air, dissipating quickly into the gusty autumn wind. The trees around the station had begun to change colour, their leaves shifting from gold to deep chocolate brown to rust. Ruth couldn't understand anyone who didn't appreciate this change, the transition from summer into autumn.

Ruth took another drag, leaning back against the car, allowing herself to simply *be* for a moment. It was rare, this sense of peace. Her life had been tumultuous in recent years – filled with cases, family drama and near-death experiences. She'd nearly lost her life after the shooting, and the subsequent months had been a blur of recovery, both physical and emotional. Still, things had settled now. Sarah and she had officially adopted Daniel, and the family had found a rhythm. Their trip to Paris for Daniel's birthday had been the highlight – a moment of happiness Ruth had never imagined possible after everything they'd endured. But there was a dark shadow in the back of her mind, an unspoken fear that her happiness was fragile and fleeting. That it would all come crashing down around her at any moment.

Her phone rang, breaking her train of thought. It was Georgie. Ruth smiled, the tension in her shoulders easing slightly at the familiar voice.

'Hi, boss,' Georgie's voice crackled over the line, warm but tinged with exhaustion. Ruth had become something of a maternal figure to Georgie, especially after her daughter Sylvie's birth.

'How are you guys doing?' Ruth asked, concern lacing her words.

'We're fine,' Georgie said, her voice lighter than usual. 'Better than fine, actually.'

Ruth raised an eyebrow. 'Why's that?'

'Sylvie slept through,' Georgie said, her pride evident.

'What?' Ruth spluttered. 'She's only three months old!'

'Well, she had a feed at two but then slept until seven. I feel amazing,' Georgie added, her relief palpable.

Ruth chuckled. 'Five hours. Good girl.'

'I was going to bring Sylvie in to meet the team today,' Georgie said, her tone casual but eager. 'A few of them have been pestering me. Is it okay if I pop in around two?'

Ruth grinned, the prospect of seeing Georgie and her baby brightening her mood. 'Yes, of course. It would be lovely to see you both.'

'I just wanted to check there wasn't much going on,' Georgie said, a hint of hesitation in her voice.

'No, we're…' Ruth paused, half-grinning. 'God, I nearly said the "Q" word.'

Georgie laughed. 'Never, ever say the "Q" word, boss.'

'No.' Ruth smirked. 'I'll see you about two then?'

CHAPTER 2

Detective Sergeant Nick Evans squatted down and buttoned up his daughter Megan's thick red wool coat.

'Let's get this done up properly, eh? It's getting cold,' he said with a smile as he swept a strand of hair from her face.

Nick, his partner Amanda and their daughter Megan had been at Chester Zoo for nearly two hours. Nick had a day off from his work as a detective at Llancastell Police Station, having worked the previous weekend. Megan was in her half term so they'd decided to drive over the border to the zoo.

Amanda looked down at them. 'Where are we going next?'

They'd pretty much ticked off all the main attractions – elephants, giraffes, the big cats and the bat cave.

'Monkeys!' exclaimed Megan with an excited little jump and flap of her hands.

Amanda shook her head. 'You don't like monkeys,' she teased their daughter.

'Yes, I do! Yes, I do,' Megan squealed as she grabbed Nick's hand and pulled him towards the monkey house which was nearby. 'Come on, Daddy. Hurry up.'

Nick gave Amanda a cheeky grin. 'Demanding, impatient. I wonder who she takes after?' he joked.

'Ha, ha,' Amanda snorted sarcastically.

As Nick gave a little skip, he and Megan held hands as they bounced along the path towards the monkey enclosure. Nick didn't think that he could be any happier if he tried.

Out of the corner of his eye, he spotted a man in his late twenties wearing a black baseball cap, Stone Island jacket and Adidas trainers.

Don't I recognise him from somewhere? he thought to himself. Something about the man unsettled him. But maybe Nick was just being paranoid.

To be fair, the man looked like a million other young scallies that he'd nicked in the past. It seemed that any male under the age of twenty-three now dressed in identical clothes. Baseball caps, black sports tops or hoodies, joggers, trainers, with virtually no variation. It was a uniform.

'What are we waiting for, silly?' Megan groaned yanking at his arm.

Deciding that he wasn't going to ruin the day by trying to work out if or how he knew the man, Nick put his arm around Megan.

'Here we go,' Nick said with a laugh as they approached the enclosure.

As they gazed at the baboons and chimpanzees swinging on ropes, Nick suddenly realised how he knew the young man. He couldn't help himself.

It was Shaun Keegan.

He was a known associate of Curtis Blake and the Croxteth Park Boyz, a fearsome Organised Criminal Gang – OCG – from Liverpool. Nick had engineered Blake's murder in prison a while ago, but there were still members of the gang out there.

Before Blake's death, Nick and him went way back – nearly two decades of pure, undiluted, mutual loathing. Blake ruled Liverpool's drug scene with a psychotic grin and a reputation for violence. Imports from the Netherlands, factories, Glasgow cousins – he'd built his empire on blood and narcotics. But he was gone now. Thank God.

But that didn't stop Nick thinking of Blake every once in a while. The sunbed tan. The fake Hollywood teeth. The cars, the yacht, the villa and smug swagger.

But now Curtis Blake was finally out of the picture. Permanently.

The question was, what was Shaun Keegan doing here? Was he really on an innocent trip at Chester Zoo?

Or had someone discovered Nick's role in Blake's death? And were they out for revenge?

CHAPTER 3

Sitting back on her padded office chair, Ruth looked at the mountain of paperwork on her desk.

So much for everything going paperless and digital, she thought sardonically.

Then she looked outside at the CID team, most of whom were either working on computers or on their phones. Although they hadn't had what she would have termed 'a major incident' for several months, there were always ongoing investigations that needed looking at.

Detective Constable Jade Kennedy appeared at the open door and looked at her.

'Jade?' Ruth said sitting up in her chair and trying to pretend that she was actually hard at work. 'How can I help?'

'I just need your signature on this forensic stuff for those robberies in Ruthin,' she explained as she passed the request forms over to Ruth to sign.

Ruth scribbled what could barely pass for her signature and handed them back.

'Thanks,' Jade said.

Ruth gestured to the door. 'Just close the door a second for me, Jade, and come and sit down.' Ruth pointed to a nearby chair.

'Okay,' Kennedy said hesitantly. She looked anxious.

'Don't worry. It's nothing to worry about,' Ruth reassured her, feeling a little guilty that her clandestine request hadn't been phrased better.

'Right,' Kennedy said sitting down and peering at her. Kennedy had joined them from the Cheshire Police Force several months ago and since then, Ruth had been incredibly impressed with her work. She was meticulous and thorough, with an instinct for what made a good copper.

'Ever thought about doing your Sergeants' exams?' Ruth asked leaning forward on her chair.

Kennedy shrugged. 'A few times. It's definitely something I intend to do some time in the future.' Then she arched an eyebrow. 'Why do you ask?'

'This department needs at least one more DS going forward,' Ruth explained.

'I always thought that Georgie would be moving up the ladder before I did,' Kennedy admitted.

'I think Georgie is going to be pretty busy for the next couple of years,' Ruth said with a wry expression. 'Have a think about it, Jade. I'm more than happy to put a recommendation in for you. And it's more money.'

Kennedy gave her a half-smile. 'Yeah, there is that.' Then she nodded. 'I'll definitely give it some thought in the next few days, if that's all right?'

'More than all right,' Ruth stated but something in the corner of her eye attracted her attention.

It was Detective Sergeant Jim Garrow.

He gave her a look through the glass of the door to suggest that whatever he needed to talk to her about was urgent.

Ruth got up both as a signal that her conversation with Georgie was now over and so that she could find out why Jim needed to speak to her.

'Thanks, Jade,' Ruth said with a kind expression as Kennedy left and headed back towards her desk. Ruth was pretty confident that after their conversation, Kennedy would decide to make the application for her Sergeants' exams. Ruth was just surprised that it wasn't something that Kennedy had considered before.

'Boss,' Garrow said.

'What's up, Jim?' Ruth asked. She was glad to see that in recent weeks Garrow – or *Prof*, as some of the CID team called him because of his university degree and intellectual way of speaking and tackling investigations – was back to his old self.

Garrow had been to hell and back in the past six months. It had started when a woman called Lucy Morgan had been found at the Pontcysyllte Aqueduct claiming to have amnesia on the night that her mother, Lynne Morgan, was brutally murdered at her home in

Wrexham. Garrow's investigation had eventually discovered that Lucy had slashed her mother's throat after a heated argument and then faked her amnesia to cover her tracks.

However, the major spanner in the works was that Garrow and Lucy had formed a romantic attachment after Lucy had been ruled out as a suspect earlier in the investigation. Although they hadn't slept together, Garrow had been to Lucy's flat. And during the trial, she had claimed they'd had sex. Her defence team had called for a mistrial due to the allegations and the judge had agreed. It was a complete disaster.

'Report of an incident over at Bangor Town Hall, boss,' Garrow explained.

'Remind me what's going on over at Bangor Town Hall this afternoon?' Ruth asked furrowing her brow. The menopause had a lot to answer for as her short-term memory seemed almost non-existent. Or maybe that was just old age.

'Ashwin Choudary is giving a speech as part of the Bangor Festival of Words,' Garrow said.

Ruth had met the MP for Bangor on several occasions and found him to be very charming, intelligent and passionate about the constituency that he represented. However, Ruth was aware that there had been several death threats from far-right extremists. Not only was Choudary an Asian MP, he had also been ferocious in his condemnation of several far-right groups. Ruth had liaised with the Counter Terrorism Unit across the border in Manchester but they were confident that such threats to Choudary's life were hollow. That's why Garrow's appearance was now making her feel uneasy.

'Yes,' Ruth remembered with an affirmative nod of her head.

'We've had reports of an incident over there,' Garrow explained.

Ruth didn't like the sound of that one bit. 'What kind of incident?' she asked anxiously.

Garrow shook his head. 'Details are very sketchy I'm afraid, boss. The initial report said that a couple of far-right extremists had tried to disrupt the event.'

Ruth nodded, hoping that it was nothing more serious than that. 'Okay, Jim, thank you. Can you keep me posted?'

'Of course,' Garrow said.

A figure appeared behind him.

It was Georgie and she was carrying her baby – Sylvie – in a baby car seat.

'Aw, here they are,' Ruth said as she went over and gave Georgie a hug. Then she squatted down to look at Sylvie who was fast asleep under a white crocheted blanket. She looked so innocent and vulnerable.

Members of the CID team came over and generally cooed.

Ruth and Georgie moved to one side for a moment.

'Where's Nick?' Georgie asked.

'Day off,' Ruth replied. 'I think they've gone to the zoo.'

'Aw, that's nice.'

'More importantly, how are things going with Adam?' Ruth asked quietly. She wasn't sure that Georgie necessarily wanted her relatively new relationship with the hunky paramedic, who had moved in next door to her about three months ago, broadcast to the world.

Georgie looked puzzled. 'He's been amazing. When he's not on a shift, he's in my house cleaning up, making up bottles, changing nappies.'

Ruth raised an eyebrow. 'I get the feeling there's a "but" coming?'

'Not really.' Georgie pulled a face. 'I just worry that he's just too good to be true. I keep thinking that at some point he's going to reveal his dark, horrible side. But he doesn't.'

Ruth gave here a half-smile of recognition. 'I know that feeling. When things are going too well, I just instinctively start to worry.'

Georgie laughed. 'Exactly.'

Ruth put a comforting hand on Georgie's shoulder as they watched everyone fussing over Sylvie. 'Hey, just enjoy it. You've been through a lot in the last eighteen months. You deserve a bit of good luck.'

Ruth then spotted Garrow heading their way with a sombre expression. Ruth's mind went back to what he'd told her about Ashwin Choudary.

'Sorry to break up the party, boss,' Garrow said apologetically.

'What is it?' Ruth asked.

'Ashwin Choudary has been shot,' Garrow explained.

Ruth shook her head. 'How bad is it?'

'Bad,' Garrow admitted. 'The air ambulance has just landed but it doesn't look good. They're not sure he's going to make it.'

CHAPTER 4

Ruth and Kennedy were hammering across Snowdonia as they made their way towards Bangor. The grey cloud cover hung low, oppressive, dragging mist like a torn veil across the hills. It had sucked every ounce of colour from the world, leaving the fields sallow and the distant slopes washed in cold ash tones.

'Mind if I smoke?' Ruth asked Kennedy who was staring intently at the road ahead.

Kennedy gave a little shake of her head which was unconvincing but Ruth needed to smoke so that was that.

Buzzing down the window, Ruth was hit by the cold, damp, fungoid odour from outside. She pulled out a cigarette and popped it in her mouth.

'I don't follow politics,' Kennedy admitted. 'But I can't remember a time when far-right groups were this powerful or dangerous.'

Ruth lit her cigarette, took a drag and then blew the smoke out of the window. She wasn't sure. It was definitely getting worse in recent years. 'The late Seventies were pretty bad where I lived in London. National Front skinheads were very scary. It was all tied into football hooliganism.'

Kennedy shrugged. 'Before my time. But my mum told me about being spat at by skinheads when she was younger and living in South London.'

'Jesus…' Ruth groaned but then her phone rang. It was Nick. She'd sent him a message to give her call.

'Boss?' Nick said. 'Everything okay?'

'Ashwin Choudary's been shot. At an event in Bangor,' Ruth said, voice taut.

'How bad?' Nick asked.

'Bad. Air Ambulance is already on scene.'

Nick didn't answer straight away. You could almost hear the gears turning.

'Right,' he said at last.

'I know it's your day off, but if this turns into murder...'

'I'm there,' Nick cut in. 'We're heading home anyway.'

'Good. How's Megan?' Ruth softened just a touch as her godmother mode kicked in.

'She's good. We needed the break, so it was... nice,' Nick said. 'Keep me posted.'

'Will do.' Ruth ended the call and exhaled, long and slow. 'I hate making those calls,' she muttered.

'Comes with the badge,' Kennedy said as Bangor's welcome sign loomed, *Croeso*. The cathedral, the university, the pier – all lined up in blue and white.

'Here we go,' Ruth said as she finished her cigarette and wound up her window. Then she glanced over at the satnav which showed them where Penrhyn Hall was.

There was a sudden noise. A deep mechanical vibrating that got louder.

Looking up, Ruth spotted the Welsh Air Ambulance, which was bright red with a green pattern that swirled back towards the tail, lifting up into the air.

A few seconds later, they turned into the road where Penrhyn Hall was located. The whole area was a sea of flashing blue lights and high-vis jackets. Police officers had already taped off the whole area and were making sure that members of the public were being kept back.

'Bloody hell,' Ruth said under her breath as Kennedy parked up on the pavement.

Getting out, the air was filled with a crackling noise of police and emergency service radios.

Ruth and Kennedy approached a young male uniformed police officer – twenties, blond, wiry.

'DI Ruth Hunter and DC Jade Kennedy, Llancastell CID,' she explained as they flashed their warrant cards. 'Who's in charge here, Constable?'

The young police officer pointed to a woman in her forties who was deep in conversation with several other officers and a paramedic.

'Sergeant Dixon is, ma'am,' the constable replied.

Kennedy looked at him. 'Any idea of the extent of Ashwin Choudary's injuries?'

The constable gave them a dark look. 'According to the paramedics, very serious.'

Ruth's mind was whirring. Her instinct was that Choudary might die from his injuries. And if that happened, she would be dealing with a homicide case. And a very high profile one given that Choudary was an MP. Therefore, she had to act as if this was a murder investigation from now on.

'I'm going to need you to run a scene log please, Constable,' Ruth explained as she pointed to the dozens of people milling around. 'I want everyone away from the building. This is a major crime scene. Only senior ranking police officers and the forensic team inside from now on.'

'Got it, ma'am,' the constable said nervously. It was as if the gravity of the situation had just hit him.

'Thank you, Constable,' Ruth said as he lifted the blue and white police tape so that they could proceed.

They headed over towards where Sergeant Dixon was standing. She spotted them and gave them a quizzical look.

'DI Ruth Hunter and DC Jade Kennedy, Llancastell CID,' Ruth said evenly, flipping open her warrant card for the second time.

Sergeant Dixon gave it a cursory glance, her expression curdling into something between suspicion and contempt. 'Right. CID.'

Here we go, Ruth thought, suppressing a sigh. She'd dealt with plenty of Dixons before. Uniformed sergeants who bristled the moment CID stepped in. It wasn't new. But it was always tedious.

The unwritten battle lines were familiar. CID swept into a scene and, more often than not, took over. It didn't matter how much groundwork Uniform had already put in – suddenly it was all hands off, let the detectives take the glory. She'd seen that resentment run deep in London, especially when fresh-faced CID men turned up acting like they were in an episode of *Line of Duty*.

Still, Ruth made a conscious effort to temper her tone. 'What have we got, Sergeant?' she asked, adopting a level, professional voice. One that suggested collaboration rather than command.

Dixon didn't seem convinced. 'Ashwin Choudary was giving a talk. Part of the Bangor Festival of Words which begins this weekend,' she began, her voice clipped. 'Two men started heckling him mid-speech. My officers moved in, tried to get them out quietly. It turned into a scuffle. Then one of those men'—she nodded towards the hall, still surrounded by tape and chaos'—ran forward, pulled a gun, and shot him twice before running off.'

Kennedy raised an eyebrow. 'We heard that you had someone in custody?'

Dixon jerked her thumb towards a marked car parked just beyond the cordon. Inside, a man in his forties sat slumped in the backseat, his face barely visible behind steamed-up windows.

'We got the second guy. My officers managed to pin him down just as he tried legging it through the crowd,' Dixon said. 'He's not saying very much.'

'Any ID on him?' Ruth asked, scanning the perimeter with sharp eyes.

'Not a scrap. No wallet, no phone. Nothing but attitude.' Dixon gave a humourless snort.

Ruth's mind immediately went to the Counter Terrorist Division in Manchester. If this had the hallmarks of a far-right hit – and it was beginning to look that way – they'd need intel fast. The CTD could dig up more in an hour than CID could in a day when it came to extremist networks.

Kennedy, already scribbling in her notebook, piped up. 'Any idea how the shooter escaped?'

Dixon pointed down the road with a jerk of her head. 'A black scooter. Witnesses say he took off like a bat out of hell. It was stashed down near the side alley, off Penrhyn Street.'

'Did anyone get a registration?' Ruth asked, not hopeful.

Dixon shook her head. 'Of course not. But my officers are taking statements from everyone who was inside the hall. We're also canvassing across the road to check if anyone saw anything useful.'

Ruth glanced up instinctively and spotted a security camera mounted high on the building opposite the hall – its blinking red light still on.

'Jade. Looks like CCTV. That one, there,' she pointed. 'Can we get someone on it ASAP.'

Kennedy nodded. 'Will do, boss.'

As Ruth turned back to Dixon, a flicker of movement caught her eye. Two paramedics were approaching, one of them older, heavy-set with a greying beard and eyes that telegraphed bad news before he even opened his mouth.

'Sergeant,' the man began grimly.

Dixon stepped forward. 'CID', she said flatly, motioning to Ruth and Kennedy as if they were a necessary inconvenience.

The paramedic gave a nod, lips tightening. 'Right. I've had a call from our air ambulance team. I'm sorry to say that Mr Choudary didn't make it. He died en route.'

A sharp silence fell over them.

Ruth barely blinked, but something heavy settled in her chest.

Kennedy looked up from her notebook, expression flickering for just a second.

Dixon muttered something under her breath, barely audible. 'Jesus Christ.'

Ruth turned to her. 'We'll need full access to your officers' statements, scene logs and bodycam footage, if they were wearing any.'

Dixon crossed her arms. 'Of course. Wouldn't want to get in CID's way.'

Ruth met her gaze, unfazed. 'I'm glad we agree.'

CHAPTER 5

Nick sat opposite a visibly shaken young police constable in his twenties. They were alone on one side of a cavernous, high-ceilinged meeting room inside Penrhyn Hall, where sound echoed faintly off pale blue walls. The space was orderly, furnished in dark mahogany and burgundy leather. The air smelled faintly of dust and old paper, that dry, nostalgic scent of a rarely disturbed library.

'Constable Stu Adams,' the young man said quietly, as Nick scribbled the name into his notebook.

Nick had dropped Amanda and Megan back at the cottage before hammering across the rugged miles of Snowdonia to Bangor. He hadn't even had time to change his clothes so he was still wearing the thick navy roll-neck jumper he'd worn to the zoo, jeans, worn trainers crusted with gravel. He didn't look like a senior CID officer.

'And where are you based, Stu?' Nick asked, keeping his tone even.

Stu drew in a shaky breath, the kind you take when you're still forcing your heart to slow. He was one of the officers who'd taken down the two young far-right extremists just before Ashwin Choudary had been shot dead. His split lip was a raw gash against otherwise pale skin.

He blinked slowly, jaw working like he was grinding back emotion.

'I'm with the North Gwynedd Response Unit,' he said at last. 'Based in Caernarfon.'

Nick nodded but didn't speak yet.

'Sorry I...' Stu mumbled apologetically.

Nick leaned forward. 'It's okay, Stu. You take your time. You've just witnessed a shooting. You're bound to be pretty shaken up.'

Stu gave Nick a nod. He seemed relieved and reassured by Nick's words. He then pointed over to a large window. 'I'm currently based at Bangor Police Station. It's literally round the corner from here,' he explained with a dark irony.

'And when did you first become aware of these two men?' Nick asked.

Stu thought for a moment and scratched at his nose. 'I guess it was a few minutes after Mr Choudary had started to talk. They started booing and shouting stuff over at him.'

Nick nodded. 'Can you remember what they were shouting?'

'*You're a disgrace*. And *Rights for Whites*. That type of thing,' Stu replied. 'And they shouted about immigrants.'

'Can you talk me through what happened,' Nick said.

'Sergeant Wilkinson and I moved towards the men. We were going to escort them out of the building,' Stu said. 'A couple of people turned, told them to shut up and a fight broke out. Sergeant Wilkinson and I went over to break it up.'

Nick pointed over to Stu's lip. 'And that's when you got that?'

'Yeah,' Stu nodded. 'The older man just punched me. And then I tried to tackle the younger man but he overpowered me...' Stu stopped.

'It's okay,' Nick said quietly.

'And then he ran towards the stage, pulled out a firearm and shot Mr Choudary twice,' Stu said in a virtual whisper. 'I keep thinking, if only I'd managed to stop him...'

'He had a gun. Anything could have happened,' Nick said, trying to allay his guilt. 'He could have shot you or your colleague.'

Stu nodded but he didn't seem convinced by what Nick had said.

Nick stopped writing and glanced over. 'I've seen the older man who has been arrested but can you describe the younger man who fired the gun?'

'Late twenties. Average build. Short blond hair. He had a British Bulldog with a Union Jack tattooed on his right upper arm. And then on his other arm he had *Stoke City FC – Naughty 40*.'

Nick raised an eyebrow. He didn't know what that meant. 'Naughty Forty?'

Stu nodded. 'Yeah, it's the name of the Stoke City hooligan gang. Nasty bastards.'

'Right.' Nick narrowed his eyes and he wrote this down. It was a significant piece of evidence.

He closed his notebook slowly, the click of the clasp loud in the silence.

He was getting the feeling that this wasn't just a random act – it was orchestrated. And somewhere out there, the next move was already being planned.

CHAPTER 6

It had been an hour since Ruth had returned to Llancastell nick. The unidentified man who had been arrested at the shooting in Bangor was now sitting downstairs in a holding cell in custody. He was refusing to answer any questions and had no ID, phone or any way of them knowing who he was.

Rain had begun to fall again, tapping lightly against the grimy sash windows of her office. Outside, the grey slate roofs of Llancastell were slick with water, glistening under a dull pewter sky. Somewhere in the distance, the low growl of the swirling wind.

Garrow appeared at the door and gave it a little knock. 'Boss, I've got DCI Robert Murphy from the Special Crime and Counter Terrorism Division in Manchester on the line. Shall I put him through?'

'Please,' Ruth replied. 'Thanks, Jim.'

A few seconds later, the phone on her desk buzzed. Ruth had already had dealings with DCI Rob Murphy when British Action, the far-right terrorist group, had first made death threats towards Ashwin Choudary. She found Rob to be a very calm, intelligent officer and easy to deal with – which wasn't always the case with some of the anti-terrorist units that she'd dealt with in the past.

'Rob,' Ruth said in a suitably solemn tone as she picked up the phone.

'Hi, Ruth,' Rob sighed. 'I can't believe they've done this.'

By *they*, Rob meant British Action.

'Neither can I,' Ruth admitted.

'Who was Gold Command for the event in Bangor?' Rob asked.

'Bangor Police were in charge over there,' Ruth said, thankful that she hadn't been given the task. An MP had been murdered, so there was going to be a very thorough inquiry – every risk assessment dissected, every officer's decision under a microscope. How had a far-right extremist smuggled a gun into the town hall? And why hadn't the warning signs – because there were always warning signs – been seen?

'I guess the IOPC are going to be all over this like a rash,' Rob said.

The IOPC – the Independent Office for Police Conduct – was the public body responsible for handling serious complaints against the police forces in England and Wales.

'And the press is going to have a field day if it comes out that there had been threats to Ashwin's life,' Ruth said wearily, rubbing the tension from her brow with the edge of her palm.

'What a shitshow,' Rob groaned. 'I hear you've got one of them in custody?'

'Yes. No ID and he's not talking,' Ruth explained.

'I've got photos here of all the main members of British Action if you want me to send it over now?' Rob suggested.

'That would be great,' Ruth said gratefully, glancing at the clock on the wall. 'I'd like to interview him around five. Does that work for you?'

'I'll try to get to you by four, at a push. I'm bringing DS Jane Robinson with me. Has the suspect lawyered up or is he taking the duty solicitor?'

'I've no idea at the moment,' Ruth admitted. 'He's not responding to anything. But unless someone turns up, the duty solicitor will be in with us.'

'Okay. I've just sent that photo sheet over now,' Rob said. 'Do you want to have a look while I'm on the phone?'

'Good idea,' Ruth said as she opened her email and clicked on Rob's attachment.

Her screen was filled with a dozen or so faces of the prominent members of British Action. What had always surprised Ruth when she'd first come across the far-right extremists was how many of the prominent members didn't look like your archetypal knuckle-dragging, neo-Nazi thug.

The leader of British Action, Neil Baker, was a handsome man in his forties with greying hair and a sharp navy suit. He looked more like he belonged in a boardroom than at the helm of a hate group. His second in command, Gary Bentley, wore thick-framed glasses and had a scholarly, almost gentle air – apart from the close-cropped hair and steel-eyed stare.

Then, in the bottom right-hand corner of the screen, Ruth saw a photo of a man in his fifties. Coal-black hair swept back, three-day stubble, and deep-set brown eyes that were hooded and watchful.

That's him.

Raymond Clarke.

Ruth double-checked the image and leaned back in her chair.

'Raymond Clarke. That's the man we've got down in custody, Rob.'

'Right,' Rob responded after a pause. 'We don't have much on him. He's listed as a foot soldier in British Action. Recently married a Sheila Clarke. Two kids from a previous marriage. Works nights at a petrol station in Stoke. Keeps his head down.'

'Until today.'

'Yeah. Until today,' Rob echoed with a sigh.

There was silence for a moment.

'We've got a trace on Clarke's car,' Rob continued. 'It was picked up on ANPR leaving Stoke yesterday afternoon. But here's the thing – we didn't have him flagged. No watch list. Nothing to suggest Clarke would do something like this.'

'Maybe he didn't know,' Ruth said, voice tightening. 'Maybe the shooter was acting alone.'

Rob cleared his throat, his voice slightly lowered. 'There's one more thing you should know. They've started referring to someone as *Wolf* in the last year or so.'

'Wolf?' Ruth's brow furrowed.

'Yeah. No confirmed ID, no photo, no real intel beyond the name. But apparently, *Wolf* is the one pulling the strings behind British Action. The rest of them – Baker, Bentley, Clarke – they're loud, visible, easy enough to track. But this person...' he trailed off. 'They've kept themselves entirely off radar.'

Ruth gave a sharp, withering sigh. 'Of course they have. Let me guess – the whole codename thing is supposed to be intimidating?'

Rob gave a dry laugh, devoid of humour. 'Actually, it's ideological. "Adolf" in German – it means *Noble Wolf*. So it was Hitler's favourite animal, apparently.'

Ruth shook her head, a bitter twist at the corner of her mouth. 'Jesus. It's like they're all playing dress-up with fascist folklore.'

'Well, Wolf, whoever they are, seems to operate from the shadows. We've had whispers. A couple of encrypted chat groups, second-hand accounts. But nothing we can pin down. Meanwhile, our eyes stay fixed on Baker and Bentley, while the one who might actually matter disappears into smoke. But don't worry, we'll find him,' he said in a determined tone. 'Even shadows leave footprints, if you know where to look.'

CHAPTER 7

Thirty minutes later, Ruth had called a briefing for the whole of the Llancastell CID team. She'd already had a phone call from her superintendent warning her that he was under pressure from the top brass in the North Wales Police to deliver results in the investigation and fast. Ruth had also had a call from the North Wales Police media office based in St Asaph asking her to run a press conference.

Blowing out her cheeks, Ruth grabbed her coffee and files and proceeded out of her office into the main hub of Llancastell CID.

'Right, everyone,' she said as she strode across the room towards the scene boards which had now been set up on the far side. 'If we can listen up, please.'

At its centre was a photo of Ashwin Choudary with a beaming smile on the night he won his seat in the 2017 general election. His date of birth – 3.5.67 – was scribbled underneath, along with other details.

Ruth took a moment to look at the photo, then turned to face the CID team. 'As you're all aware, Ashwin Choudary, MP for Bangor Aberconwy, was shot and killed at an event in Bangor a few hours ago.' Ruth went to the photo and tapped her index finger against it. 'Ashwin had dedicated his life to serving his community, firstly as a teacher, then a local counsellor and finally as an MP. This was a brutal, senseless killing so I want us all to do our best work to get justice for him and his family.' Ruth pointed to another photo. 'We know that two men who we believe were members of the far-right terrorist group British Action attended the event today. They started to heckle Ashwin, a fight broke out, and two local uniformed officers moved in to break it up. One of the men charged towards the stage and shot Ashwin twice with a handgun. Sadly, even though paramedics worked on Ashwin as he was being airlifted to the local trauma centre, he died from his injuries en route.' Ruth moved across the scene board and pointed to another photo. 'Okay. We now know this man, Raymond Clarke, was one of those men but he wasn't the man with the gun. Clarke is downstairs in custody and I'll be interviewing him alongside DCI Robert Murphy from the CPS Special Crime and Counter Terrorism Division in Manchester. We also have a DS Jane Robinson coming from that unit to work with us.'

'Does Clarke have a solicitor?' Garrow asked.

Ruth shook her head. 'No. I've instructed the duty solicitor to be present.'

A duty solicitor, usually criminally trained, was someone who was available at police stations and courts to provide free legal advice to those who couldn't afford to hire their own solicitor.

Ruth continued. 'Clarke is refusing to talk to us and he may well go for a "no comment" interview.' She then gestured to the printout of the main members of British Action that DCI Murphy had sent over to her. 'Counter Intelligence have sent us these photos of prominent members of the group. You can see Clarke down here. DCI Murphy thinks that Clarke is no more than a foot soldier. I've sent this over to Bangor nick for the two uniformed officers to look at. Frustratingly, the man that shot Ashwin doesn't appear to be any of these men... Nick?'

Nick got up and went to the board. 'Okay. We know that the shooter left Penrhyn Hall and then used a black scooter to make his escape. We're still waiting for the CCTV from the building opposite. Hopefully we can get a look at the registration.'

Kennedy signalled she had something to say. 'I've been on to Traffic. They're looking at all the cameras around Bangor to see if they can spot the scooter.'

'Good,' Nick said. 'If we can trawl through the eye-witness statements to see if there's anything significant. Constable Stu Adams noticed that our shooter had a *Naughty 40* tattoo. Apparently, they are the Stoke City Football hooligan firm. Someone get onto Staffordshire Police and see what intel they have on known Stoke City hooligans. Give them our description and see if we can get a match.'

'Jesus,' Kennedy sighed under her breath. She was looking at her computer screen.

Ruth arched an eyebrow. 'What is it?'

'A post on the British Action website,' Kennedy explained as she turned the monitor to show everyone. 'It reads *This is just the first blow. Only 649 MPs to go.*'

Ruth shook her head in disbelief. Then she got her head back into Detective Inspector mode. 'Okay, everyone. I want us to pull Clarke's phone and bank records. Trawl his social media. Look at anyone he was talking to in the last few weeks.'

Garrow looked over. 'Boss. The petrol station that he works at in Stoke has CCTV. I've told them to send over everything they've got. It might be that the shooter was there at some point if they needed to talk?'

'Good point,' Nick agreed.

Ruth looked out at the CID team. 'Right, everyone. Let's get cracking. Prioritise CCTV trawls throughout Bangor. Chase ANPR hits. No assumptions and no shortcuts. And let's get justice for Ashwin Choudary and his family.'

CHAPTER 8

Half an hour later, Ruth and DCI Rob Murphy were making their way along the ground floor of Llancastell nick towards Interview Room 2 where Raymond Clarke had been taken to be interviewed.

Rob looked at his phone as they went and shook his head. 'The Mail Online are already spinning the line of police incompetence. Which is a bit rich as Ashwin Choudary was one of their main targets in recent years.'

Ruth winced. 'I think it's only going to get worse,' she sighed.

'Obviously we need to find out the identity of the gunman. But what I really want is to get the bastards at the top of British Action,' Rob admitted. 'The ones that planned and gave the orders. Not a brainless soldier like Clarke.'

Ruth nodded in agreement. 'Yeah. They can replace Clarke just like that,' she said with a little click of her fingers.

Rob looked at her. 'You think he's going to talk?'

'No, I don't.' Ruth shook her head. 'I'm sure that it was drummed into Clarke and the shooter that if they got caught, they should say nothing and answer every question "no comment".'

They arrived at Interview Room 2 and stopped outside.

'And I'm also pretty sure that it was made clear to them what the consequences would be of co-operating with us in any way,' Rob said with a grim expression.

'And Clarke has got a wife and two children,' Ruth said under her breath as she opened the door and they went in.

Clarke was now dressed in a grey sweatshirt and bottoms. His clothes had been taken for extensive DNA analysis. His mouth had been swabbed for a DNA sample and his nails clipped. His black hair was swept off his face. His face was thinner than in the photo that Ruth had seen of him. His dark eyes darted nervously over in their direction as they walked over to the other side of the table and pulled out two chairs.

Clarke then leaned in to talk to the station's duty solicitor, Neil Roberts, and whispered something in his ear.

Ruth pulled in her chair and looked over at Clarke. His leg was jiggling nervously as he stared down at the floor. Then he anxiously pushed a strand of hair from his forehead.

Wow, he looks terrified, Ruth thought to herself. It made her wonder if he would crack under the pressure of an interview and give them useful information. She thought it unlikely, but she had seen men just crumble with the strain of being in an official police interview – especially if they had little or no experience of dealing with the police.

Ruth leaned over, took her electronic tablet and made sure that it was switched on. Then she glanced at Rob who also had a police issue tablet that he had on the desk in front of him.

Ruth leaned over and pressed the red button on the digital recording equipment. There was a long, loud electronic beep.

'Interview conducted with Raymond Clarke, Interview Room 2, Llancastell Police Station. Present are Detective Chief Inspector Robert Murphy, duty solicitor Neil Roberts and myself, Detective Inspector Ruth Hunter. Time is'—she glanced at her tablet—'five twenty-three p.m.'

Rob raised his eyebrow and looked over. 'Raymond?'

Clarke looked up and blinked.

'Or is it Ray?' Rob asked.

For a second, Clarke looked confused by the question. Then he gave a little shrug. 'Ray,' he mumbled very quietly.

Ruth looked over and saw the tattoos of a swastika and a clenched fist on the back of Clarke's hands. Over the backs of his fingers on his left hand he had the letters R A I N. On his right hand, H A T E.

Not 'Love' then? Ruth thought to herself sardonically.

Rob nodded and fixed Clarke with a stare. 'Okay. Ray, do you understand that you are under arrest for conspiracy to murder and racially aggravated violent affray?'

Clarke took a moment and then shrugged. 'Yeah,' he said unconvincingly and then scratched nervously at his face.

Ruth leaned forward. 'Ray, you were arrested at Penrhyn Hall in Bangor earlier today. Can you tell us why you were there?'

Clarke's eyes dropped to the floor as he fidgeted in his seat. 'No comment,' he said in a low tone.

'Ray,' Ruth said trying to get his attention and get him to look at her. His eyes stayed firmly fixed to the floor. 'We believe that you are a member of the far-right group, British Action? Is that correct?'

Clarke took a deep breath. 'No comment.'

'Are you aware that British Action is a proscribed terrorist group under the Terrorism Act of 2000?' Ruth asked in flat tone.

Clarke didn't respond.

'For the purposes of the recording, the suspect has not responded to that question,' Rob said.

Silence.

Ruth waited, letting the tension build in the room, hoping that it would add to Clarke's growing anxiety.

'Are you also aware,' Ruth said eventually, 'that being a member of a proscribed group is a criminal offence under the Terrorism Act of 2000, with the penalty for membership including a prison sentence?'

'No comment,' Clarke replied in a virtual whisper.

Rob shifted in his chair with a sudden jolt, his irritation beginning to simmer beneath the surface. Ruth could see the line in his jaw harden, his patience thinning.

'Ray, I'm going to tell you what I think happened today,' Rob said in a sharp tone. 'You and your mate went along to this event where Ashwin Choudary was speaking, to cause a bit of trouble. You planned to shout a few things at him, disrupt the event and maybe get some press coverage, isn't that right?'

Rob waited for a few seconds. Clarke leaned forward, staring intently at the floor and ran his hands through his hair. Ruth could see that his hands were trembling slightly – he was clearly struggling with the pressure of being interviewed.

'What you didn't know,' Rob continued, 'was that your mate was going to pull out a gun and shoot Ashwin Choudary dead. That's right, isn't it?'

Clarke frowned and then looked over at the duty solicitor, Roberts. Then he leaned in and they had a whispered conversation for about a minute.

It was a smart move to suggest that Clarke knew nothing of the plan to shoot and kill Ashwin Choudary. It gave him a way out.

'No comment,' Clarke said looking over at them uncertainly.

Ruth narrowed her eyes. 'You see, at this moment, Ray, you are charged with conspiracy to murder. That carries a life sentence. And given that this was a planned assassination of a Westminster MP, racially motivated, and a firearm was used, a judge might decide to give you a whole life tariff.'

Clarke looked very confused. He clearly had no idea what 'a whole life tariff' meant. He leaned in again to talk to Roberts who clearly explained that 'a whole life tariff' meant exactly that. He could spend the rest of his life in prison.

The colour suddenly drained from Clarke's face.

'And if not,' Rob said, 'you'd be looking at thirty to thirty-five years behind bars. You'd be an old man by the time you got out.'

Ruth tapped at her tablet to check on some intel she had stored there. 'You're recently married, aren't you, Ray? Sheila? And your kids are Alfie and Chelsie?'

Clarke didn't answer her. But his face couldn't hide how much what they'd explained had unsettled him.

Ruth looked at Rob. 'I guess that they'll be middle-aged by the time you get out.'

Rob nodded. 'You'll be a grandad by then, Ray.'

'And of course it would be hard to guess what Sheila will be doing when that day comes,' Ruth said almost to herself.

'Probably with someone else by then,' Rob said to Ruth.

The psychological games were beginning to take root.

For a few seconds, there was silence in the room.

Clarke's mind was clearly spinning with everything that Ruth and Rob had told him. And Ruth's instinct was that Clarke wasn't intelligent enough to know how difficult it would be for them to prove joint enterprise against him. And with the huge issue of prison overcrowding in the UK, whatever sentence Clarke was given, he was likely to only serve half. And with good behaviour, that could even be reduced down to 40 per cent these days.

'Okay,' Clarke whispered almost imperceptibly. He sounded defeated.

Ruth gave Rob a cursory glance. Was Clarke about to co-operate with their investigation? It certainly sounded like it.

Clarke then looked over at them and gave a sigh. He then leaned in to talk to the duty solicitor. It certainly looked as if he'd made some kind of decision.

Ruth and Rob waited as Roberts nodded and gave Clarke his advice. They stopped talking.

Roberts gave them a meaningful look and said, 'My client would like to…'

There was a knock at the door and Roberts stopped.

The door then opened and a uniformed officer looked in. There was a grey-haired man in an expensive suit standing beside her.

'I'm very sorry, ma'am,' the female officer said pulling a face. 'But Mr Jefferson insisted that I interrupt.'

'Yes,' Jefferson said as he strode into the room with a confidence that bordered on arrogance. 'Patrick Jefferson. I will now be taking over as Mr Clarke's legal counsel, so I insist that you halt this interview until I've had a chance to speak to my client.'

Jesus, Ruth thought in frustration. *You've got to be joking.*

Rob gave her a withering look. If Ruth was to guess, Patrick Jefferson's legal services would have been retained by British Action, who had some very wealthy backers. And Jefferson sounded and looked like his services weren't cheap.

'Interview suspended at five forty-one p.m.,' Ruth said reluctantly as she reached over and pressed the button on the digital recording equipment.

Rob got up from his chair with a face like thunder. They had been seconds away from Clarke agreeing to co-operate. It was very likely that Jefferson would strongly suggest that Clarke stick to 'no comment', especially bearing in mind who was paying for Jefferson's services.

'I'd like us to come back in here in an hour,' Ruth said to Jefferson as she stood up.

Jefferson gave her a pompous look. 'I'll let you know when we're ready and my client is available to be interviewed again.'

What a wanker, Ruth thought.

She followed Rob out into the corridor. Neither of them spoke for a moment.

'How long do you think Jefferson's been lurking for that entrance?' Rob asked, his voice low, bitter.

Ruth ran a hand down her face. 'Long enough to know we were making progress.'

She turned and looked back through the small glass panel in the door. Clarke now looked small, dwarfed by the legal power suddenly standing beside him.

CHAPTER 9

Ruth sat in her office nursing her coffee, staring at a patch of damp spreading across the far wall. Rob had gone to make some phone calls while they waited for Jefferson to speak to Clarke and then inform them that he could be interviewed again. The radiator under the window hissed quietly, the only sound beside the occasional chatter from the CID office beyond.

The silence had weight.

A knock at the door.

'Boss,' said Nick, stepping in. 'Still fuming about Clarke's legal counsel?'

Ruth nodded and pinched her fingers together. 'We were this close.'

Nick offered her a sheet of paper. A face stared up at her from the printout: a man in his seventies with silver-grey hair carefully coiffed into a wave, pinstripe suit perfectly fitted, a smirk that somehow managed to be both aloof and smug.

'This is Alexander Hailes,' Nick said, his voice edged. 'Multi-millionaire from Dudley. And a suspected financial backer of British Action. Nothing that ties directly, of course. Everything laundered through dummy charities and shell companies. Quiet money. But the kind that buys bullets.'

Ruth studied the photo. She hated this part – the invisible strings that pulled men like Clarke out of cells and into safe hands. She sipped her coffee, now tepid and bitter.

'They're breeding something,' she muttered. 'These men. They're funding something we're only just beginning to see. They think they're buying this country back.'

Nick shifted. 'Unfortunately Hailes isn't just another crank. He's got real influence and power.'

A long silence hung between them, before Ruth changed tack. It was too depressing to think about where the growth of the far right might end.

'How was the zoo?'

Nick blinked, surprised. 'Good. Megan had a great time.'

But there was something in the way he said it – too quickly, too neatly.

Ruth tilted her head. 'You sure? Didn't you have a good time?'

He took a breath, as if weighing something. 'I thought I saw Shaun Keegan. Croxteth Boyz.'

The name landed like a dropped stone.

'Are you sure it was him?' she asked.

Nick nodded, but not confidently. 'Yeah, pretty sure. He was wearing a baseball cap and hoodie up, but he looked familiar. The way he glanced over as if he'd clocked me.'

'You think he was following you?'

'I don't know.' Nick hesitated. 'It could've been coincidence. It might not have been him, but it's unsettled me.'

Ruth felt a knot twist in her stomach. 'Just… stay vigilant. All the time, okay?'

'I will,' he said. But his voice had dipped, almost involuntarily.

Another knock as Kennedy looked in, brisk and purposeful.

'Boss. We've got the footage back from ANPR and traffic cams,' she explained.

She gestured over to her desk and turned without waiting.

Ruth stood up, set the coffee aside, and followed with Nick beside her. It was only mid-morning, but Ruth already felt the drag of fatigue behind her eyes.

'Here,' Kennedy said, dropping into her seat. 'It's grainy, but we've got the scooter leaving the scene.'

The screen lit up with a clip – a high angle, blurred by drizzle. A dark figure, full-face helmet came running along the pavement and mounted the scooter. They sped away, weaving through traffic and then disappeared.

Ruth leaned in, narrowing her eyes. She was going to need to start wearing glasses soon. In fact, she knew that she needed them already but vanity stopped her from getting a proper eye test. 'Can we get a reg?'

'Already on it, boss.' Kennedy nodded. 'I zoomed in as far as I could. Jim's calling the DVLA now.'

Garrow stood as if on cue, phone still in hand. 'Registered to a Darren Nesbitt.'

Nick sat at the desk beside them, typing quickly into the Police National Computer – PNC. 'Nesbitt... yep. Priors for racially aggravated assault, affray, inciting hatred. Not on the current CTD watch list, but he fits the profile.'

Ruth didn't answer immediately. She stared at the frozen frame on the screen, the scooter now just a blur of motion. Something about it unsettled her. A feeling she couldn't quite reach.

Nick frowned. 'How far does this footage follow him?'

'Across the border and as far as Nantwich. Then we lose him,' Kennedy admitted.

Garrow got up from his desk with a serious look on his face. 'Right, I've got an address for Nesbitt in Stoke-on-Trent.'

Ruth nodded as her mind began to race. 'Okay. We need to go and pick him up. And we're going to need firearms officers with us. He might well still have that gun.'

CHAPTER 10

It was nearly two hours later by the time Ruth and Nick pulled up close to the address that they'd been given for Darren Nesbitt. It was a small cul-de-sac in an area just south of Stoke city centre. Nesbitt's home was at the far end.

The property was a small, run-down bungalow. The white pebble-dashed walls were now stained. There was a pile of untidy bricks and timber on the weed-strewn driveway. In the front garden there was an old rusty bike, a black sack of rubbish and a broken washing machine.

Ruth reached for the car's Tetra radio as Nick turned off the ignition.

'Three-six to Alpha One,' she said. 'Are you receiving, over?'

'Alpha One, receiving, over,' came the deep male voice and the crackle of the radio.

'All units are now at target location,' Ruth said as she opened the passenger door. 'We are going to approach with caution. Out.'

Alpha One was the codename for the unit of North Wales Authorised Firearms Officers – AFOs – that were now sitting in a black, unmarked Mercedes van across from where they had parked.

Ruth had managed to rush through an arrest warrant and a Section 18 search warrant before they'd left Llancastell. She'd also spoken to CID at Stoke's central police station to tell them that they were coming to Stoke to make an arrest for a crime committed in North Wales.

Glancing left, she saw the two plain clothes officers from Stoke CID sitting in an unmarked BMW. She gave them a signal as she got out of the car to show that she and Nick were about to execute the arrest and search warrants at Nesbitt's home.

Nick went around to the boot of their Astra, opened it and pulled out two heavy Kevlar bulletproof vests that had POLICE HEDDLU written on them in thick white lettering.

'Here you go,' Nick said with a wry smile. 'And don't moan.'

Ruth grinned. 'I never moan. I just find these bloody things so horribly uncomfortable it's hard to concentrate on anything else.'

'Well, given what happened to you six months ago,' Nick said, sounding like a reprimanding parent, 'I suggest you get on with it as it might save your life.'

Pulling on the vest, Ruth pulled the straps to tighten it. 'Can I just remind you that I'm the senior ranking officer here,' Ruth joked.

'Just put it on,' Nick sighed with a wry smile.

Across the road, the sliding door to the AFOs' van was now opening. Four men in full black police firearms uniforms – Kevlar vests, helmets, boots, Heckler & Koch semi-automatic machine guns – jumped out.

Ruth gave the AFOs a silent signal as they walked up the road towards Nesbitt's house. Ruth had agreed that the CID officers from Stoke would stay to observe the operation and support if needed. The paperwork to allow them to be an active part of the arrest was too much of a ball-ache to try and rush through before their arrival.

Ruth could feel her pulse quicken as they approached the house slowly. She knew how quickly things could escalate. Nesbitt had a firearm and was wanted for murder.

Two of the AFOs moved down the side of the house as they headed to the back in case Nesbitt decided to make his escape.

As they got to the door, Ruth pressed the bell. There was no sound so instead she gave the door an authoritative knock and stepped back.

Silence.

The cul-de-sac was deserted and deadly still which added to the eerie atmosphere.

Ruth knocked again.

Nothing.

The wind picked up and a disused pizza box flipped over and flapped noisily.

She gave Nick a look. Either Nesbitt was gone or he was hiding inside.

Signalling to the AFOs, Ruth and Nick stepped back.

They were carrying a heavy red steel battering ram – known in the force amusingly as 'the big red key'.

Ruth gave them the nod and they smashed the front door open.

'Armed police!' they yelled loudly. 'Show yourselves. Armed police!'
Ruth and Nick followed them inside.

The house smelled of damp and weed. The hallway was a chaotic mess – cardboard boxes, old trainers strewn, plastic bags.

Moving swiftly through the ground floor, the AFOs checked each room and shouted 'Clear!' as they went.

Suddenly, out of the corner of her eye, Ruth saw a figure appear at the top of the stairs.

Shit!

Moving round, she braced herself in case it was Nesbitt with a firearm.

Instead, she saw a girl in her mid-teens – blonde, black trackies, vest top – sneering down at them.

'What the fuck are you doing?' she demanded, bleary eyed as if she'd just rolled out of bed.

One of the AFOs spun and pointed his sub-machine gun at her.

'Get down on the floor now!' he thundered loudly.

'What?' the girl snorted with a frown.

Christ, she's got some balls, Ruth though to herself.

'Now! I mean it!' the AFO bellowed as he stood on the first step of the staircase.

'Jesus Christ!' the girl groaned as she put her hands up and dropped to her knees.

The AFO moved up the staircase, the girl spat at him. 'Fucking pig!' she sneered.

With his gloved hand, he pushed her roughly to the landing floor. 'Right, so now that's you done for assaulting a police officer,' he growled as he pulled her hands behind her back and cuffed her.

'I don't give a fuck!' she screamed.

The AFO pulled the girl to her feet. 'Spit at me again and I'll put a hood over your head.'

As he led her down the stairs, Ruth looked at her. 'What's your name?'

The girl gave Ruth a withering smirk. 'No comment, Grandma.'

What a charmer.

'We're looking for Darren Nesbitt,' Nick said sternly.

'Good luck. He's long gone,' the girl laughed.

'Where's he gone?' Ruth snapped.

The girl shrugged. 'How do I know?'

Ruth looked at the AFO. 'Put her in the back of my car, please, Sergeant.'

The AFO moved the girl towards the front door.

'I haven't got any shoes on,' she said.

'Tough,' the AFO said.

The girl struggled again. 'I know my rights.'

The AFO was having none of it. 'Move it.'

Nick raised an eyebrow as he glanced at Ruth. 'Well, she's a little treat, isn't she?' he said sardonically.

An AFO came back from the kitchen. 'Ground floor is clear, ma'am. No sign of the suspect. And no sign of any firearms.'

Ruth pointed up the stairs. 'Shall we?'

The AFO walked up the stairs in front of them. 'Armed police! Show yourself!' he shouted.

Having heard nothing from the AFOs that were positioned at the back of the house, Ruth knew that Nesbitt hadn't made his escape that way. Maybe the girl was telling the truth and he was long gone. If Nesbitt had any inkling that they had the licence plate of his scooter, then he also knew that this was the address registered with the DVLA, and so it was only a matter of time before the house was raided.

They got to the narrow landing.

'Armed police!' the AFO yelled again. 'Show yourself!'

The first room to their left was a tip. Clothes and shoes piled in untidy heaps on the 'floordrobe'. The smell of weed was even stronger upstairs.

Ruth spotted an iPhone charging on a bedside cabinet. Taking out her blue forensic gloves, she snapped them on, retrieved the phone and popped it into an evidence bag.

They went in, checked the wardrobe and under the bed.

'Clear,' the AFO said.

The second bedroom was surprisingly tidy. There was a huge St George's Cross flag hung on the wall with the words *STOKE CITY ON TOUR WITH ENGLAND* across the middle. There was also photo of Hitler and a swastika stuck to the wall nearby.

Nick and Ruth walked in and looked around. There were several books about the second world war on the bedside table along with a Stoke City FC football programme.

Crouching down, Nick looked under the wardrobe. Then he reached under it and pulled out a black kit bag.

Ruth went over as he unzipped it and held it open.

Inside there was an array of weapons – a machete, a baseball bat with nails driven through it, knuckle dusters.

But no gun.

'Nice,' Nick muttered dryly.

They then checked the bathroom and a small box room that was filled with junk.

Nothing.

Ruth gave a frustrated sigh. 'If he's done a runner, then at least we can feed that registration into the ANPR system and see if we can get a hit,' she said.

They turned to head back down.

There was noise. A metallic clunk from somewhere above them.

Glancing up, Ruth saw that there was a square hatch in the ceiling which clearly led to an attic above.

Looking at the AFO, Ruth pointed up to the hatch.

The AFO nodded and moved swifty into the nearby bedroom. He returned with a chair so that he could stand on it and push up the hatch to take a look.

'Okay,' Nick said in a clear voice. 'Nesbitt's not here. He must have gone.'

'Let's go,' Ruth said.

They were hoping that if Nesbitt was hiding up there, he would lower his guard if he thought they were leaving. And that would give the AFO the element of surprise.

Standing on the chair, the AFO took a small pocket torch, turned it on and popped into his mouth so he could use both hands and hold the gun.

He then reached up with his gloved hand and very slowly pushed the hatch up.

With one swift movement, the AFO slid the hatch back, popped his head, upper torso and the gun up into the attic, and swivelled round.

Ruth held her breath and winced.

Silence.

The AFO took the torch from his mouth and looked down at them. 'Nothing up there, ma'am,' he said.

Ruth gave him a frustrated nod.

CHAPTER 11

Nick and Kennedy walked along the ground floor of Llancastell nick towards Interview Room 3. Digital Forensics had managed to get into the iPhone that Ruth had collected from the bedroom at Nesbitt's home. It belonged to Kayley Watts. A quick search on the PNC had shown that Kayley had absconded six months ago from a Shropshire care home. Even though she was only fifteen, she had a string of offences – shoplifting, petty theft, possession of drugs.

Clarke and his solicitor had finally agreed for Ruth and Rob to continue their interview with him, so it was down to Nick and Kennedy to talk to Kayley. Nick was pretty confident that Kayley was going to go 'no comment' to everything they asked but they had to go through the motions.

Opening the door, Nick saw that Kayley was now dressed in a grey sweatshirt and joggers. A woman in her fifties was sitting to one side. She was the 'appropriate adult' that Kayley had been provided with as she was only fifteen. A balding man with glasses – the duty solicitor – was sitting to her left.

Nick and Kennedy sat down opposite them.

Kayley let out a loud, withering sigh and then looked at her nails to let them know that she thought this was a massive waste of her time.

'Kayley,' Nick said looking over at her. 'I'm going to remind you that you are currently under arrest for spitting at a police officer which is a criminal offence. Do you understand that?'

Kayley continued to inspect her nails. 'No comment.'

Here we go, Nick thought to himself.

Kennedy tapped at her tablet. 'We have you registered as living at the Sunrise residential home in Telford. You were reported as missing from there three months ago. Is that correct?'

'No comment,' she said.

'We found you at an address in Stoke today that we have registered to Darren Nesbitt,' Kennedy said. 'Is that where you've been living, Kayley?'

'No comment.'

'Can you tell us what your relationship is to Darren Nesbitt,' Kennedy asked.

Kayley frowned, looked over and then pulled a face. 'Relationship? Eww. He's not a paedo.'

'Can you tell us where Darren is, Kayley?' Nick asked.

She shrugged. 'I told you. I dunno.'

Nick waited for a few seconds. They weren't getting anywhere so he needed to try and different tack.

'You understand that Darren is in very serious trouble?' Nick asked leaning forward in his chair.

Kayley shrugged but didn't say anything.

Kennedy nodded and gave Kayley a meaningful look. 'We want to speak to him in connection with a murder which took place yesterday?'

Kayley's expression froze. She clearly had no idea what they were talking about. 'Nah. You've got that all wrong. Darren ain't like that.'

Nick narrowed his eyes. 'The problem you've got is that if you know where he is, you could be aiding and abetting a murderer. And that carries a lengthy prison sentence.'

'Double digits,' Kennedy added.

The blood drained from Kayley's face. She shook her head anxiously and then turned to the duty solicitor. She leaned in, clearly to confirm what they were telling her was correct.

Then she visibly took a deep breath.

'I'm not a grass,' Kayley said as if she was building up to telling them something but wanted to pre-empt it with that insistence.

'No,' Kennedy said in a reassuring tone. 'You're not.'

Kayley then paused for a few seconds. She blinked as her eyes moved restlessly. 'Darren's brother lives up on the coast.'

'Do you know where?' Nick asked.

'Prestatyn,' she said quietly. 'Static caravan but I don't know where. I swear.'

Kennedy looked at her. 'What's his name?' she asked gently.

'Kevin,' she said in a virtual whisper. Then she looked at them both. 'But I didn't tell you this, okay?'

Nick nodded. 'No. This stays between us.'

CHAPTER 12

'Resumption of interview with Raymond Clarke, Interview Room 2, Llancastell Police Station. Present are Detective Chief Inspector Robert Murphy, Mr Clarke's solicitor, Patrick Jefferson, and myself, Detective Inspector Ruth Hunter. Time is'—she glanced at her tablet—'seven forty-five p.m.'

Clarke still looked very anxious as he fiddled nervously with his hands and looked down at the floor. There was no doubt that Jefferson would have been very explicit that Clarke needed to say 'no comment' to every question they asked from now on. And that on no account was he to tell them or co-operate in any way. Therefore, the burden of proof of his guilt would be placed squarely on Llancastell CID and the CPS. Ruth also suspected that Jefferson might have reminded Clarke about the kind of people who ran British Action and were funding his legal services. They were men not to be messed with. Unfortunately, that made their job so much harder than a few hours ago.

Rob tapped at his tablet and then looked over at Jefferson and then at Clarke. 'Just before our enforced break, we were explaining that you could be imprisoned for life, Ray. Do you remember that?'

'No comment,' Clarke mumbled into his chest.

There were a few seconds of silence.

'Ray,' Ruth said in a gentle tone. 'If you don't talk to us, we can't help you. I can't believe that you want to go to prison and miss out on watching Alfie and Chelsie grow up?'

Ruth let her words hang for a few more seconds.

'Come on, Ray,' Ruth sighed in an almost encouraging tone. 'You didn't know that Darren Nesbitt brought a gun with him today, did you?'

Clarke's hands were shaking and he clenched his fists and sat forward on his chair. 'No comment.' His voice trembled.

'You didn't know that Darren was going to shoot and kill Ashwin Choudary, did you?' Ruth asked quietly. 'Why should you go to prison for that? That's not fair, is it?'

Clarke's eyes roamed wildly around the room. He took a nervous glance over at Jefferson as if looking for some kind of guidance.

Rob sat back in his seat and said in a calm, chatty voice, 'Ray, you strike me as an okay kind of bloke. You work hard, support your kids and your wife. You don't like what you see going on in this country. I'm not interested in your politics. I'm not judging you for that. But you went along today to voice your opinion and your anger towards an MP. We pride ourselves on having freedom of speech in this country. But now you're looking at spending a huge amount of time in prison because you were in the wrong place at the wrong time.' Ray sat forward and tried to get Clarke to look at him. 'Ray?' Clarke looked up at him. 'In my book, that's not fair. You don't deserve that and neither does your family, do they? Why should you all suffer?'

Clarke looked as if he could hardly get his breath. But Ruth's instinct was that they had him on the ropes.

There was a knock at the door.

It opened slightly. It was Garrow and by the look on his face, it was urgent.

Ruth got up and headed across the room.

'For the purposes of the recording, DI Hunter is leaving the interview room,' Rob said as Ruth left and went outside.

'What is it?' Ruth asked.

'We got a call from Staffordshire Police,' Garrow explained. 'There was an incident at Raymond Clarke's home in Stoke.'

'What kind of incident?' Ruth asked.

'Someone posted a bullet through the letterbox,' Garrow explained.

'Jesus,' Ruth sighed. It was clearly a warning from the leaders of British Action to Clarke that his family would be targeted if he co-operated in any way.

'His wife and kids were pretty shaken up,' Garrow explained.

'I bet they were,' Ruth said. 'Thanks, Jim.'

Ruth headed back into the interview room, wondering if she could use the incident as some kind of leverage with Clarke.

Pulling out the chair, Ruth sat back down and then gave Clarke a meaningful look.

'Ray,' Ruth said softly. 'I don't want you to panic, but there has been an incident at your home in Stoke this evening. Sheila, Chelsie and Alfie are all okay and they're safe.'

Jefferson fixed Ruth with an icy stare.

'Oh, God,' Clarke gasped frantically. 'What do you mean? What happened?'

'Someone posted a bullet through the front door,' Ruth explained. 'I think we both know who was behind that. It was a warning for you not to talk to us, Ray.'

Clarke rubbed his face, trying to catch his breath as he shook. Then he looked over at Ruth. 'But they're all okay?' he asked.

'Yes. They're all okay,' she said. 'For now.'

Clarke stared directly at her and then gave a little nod. 'Okay. I'll talk to you,' he stammered.

Jefferson raised an eyebrow. 'I think my client could do with a break after this upsetting news.'

'No,' Clarke said looking at him. 'I need my family to be safe.' Then he looked over at Ruth and Rob. 'If I talk to you and tell you everything, can you make sure that me and my family are safe?'

'Yes,' Rob said reassuringly. 'I will have to talk to the CPS first. But I am certain that if you co-operate, we can relocate you and your family safely.'

Jefferson put his hand up. 'I must insist that I speak to my client before he incriminates himself.'

'No,' Clarke said shaking his head adamantly. 'I'm going to talk to them. And I don't want you to represent me anymore.'

'What?' Jefferson spluttered.

Ruth couldn't help but enjoy watching Jefferson's indignance.

Clarke looked at them, blinking nervously. 'Is that okay? Can I have the solicitor that I had when I first came in here?'

Ruth nodded. 'Yes, that's absolutely fine.'

Then she exchanged a look with Rob as if to say *Well, I wasn't expecting that!*

CHAPTER 13

'We need to get Sheila, Chelsie and Alfie Clarke into protective custody tonight,' Ruth said with a sense of urgency as she and Rob marched along the corridor towards the CID office.

'I've got a contact in the Witness Protection Unit,' Rob said, quickly taking out his phone. 'I'll call them now.'

'My guess is that as soon as Jefferson gets out of here, he'll be on the phone to those scumbags at British Action to tell them that Clarke has agreed to co-operate with us.'

Ruth and Rob went through the double doors into CID.

'Yeah, the family can't stay at their home,' Rob agreed. He put his phone to his ear and then started to walk away. 'I'll let you know how I get on.'

Nick approached. 'What happened with Clarke?'

'He's agreed to co-operate with us,' Ruth said, her head still spinning. 'We're going to have to wait until the morning so we can get the duty solicitor back in.'

'What about *his* solicitor?' Nick asked.

'Clarke sacked him.'

'Jesus. I bet that went down well,' Nick said with a wry expression. 'Where's Clarke's family?'

Nick clearly shared the same concerns that the family would now be in imminent danger.

Ruth gestured over to Rob who was having a conversation with someone on his phone on the far side of the office. 'Rob is talking to the Witness Protection Unit. They'll be taken into protective custody immediately.'

Nick nodded. 'Good.'

'Can you liaise with Stoke CID?' Ruth said. 'Explain what's happened here. Get them to put a uniform unit on Clarke's home.

I don't want one of those Neanderthals going there and burning down their house tonight as a reprisal.'

'Will do,' Nick said.

'Interview with Kayley?' Ruth asked.

'She told us that Darren Nesbitt has a brother in Prestatyn,' Nick replied. 'Lives in a static caravan but she didn't know exactly where.'

Ruth pulled a face. 'Yeah, that doesn't exactly narrow it down in Prestatyn, does it?' she said in frustration. 'Do we think Nesbitt is there?'

Nick nodded. 'She didn't say as much. But when we explained the hefty sentence for aiding and abetting a murderer, Kayley gave up that information almost immediately. My instinct is that she knew that's where Nesbitt had gone. She just didn't want to say it explicitly as that would make her a grass.'

'Okay,' Ruth said feeling a little more encouraged by what Nick had said. 'Take Jade and go up to Prestatyn. See what you can find.'

'It's going to be pretty quiet up in Prestatyn this time of year. And we've got Nesbitt's description and the details of his scooter. That should narrow it down a lot.'

'Yeah,' Ruth agreed. 'But be careful. He's desperate and he's got a firearm. Call for armed officers if you do find him.'

'No problem,' Nick said as Kennedy came over swiftly.

'Uniform unit spotted Nesbitt on his scooter on the A548 in Prestatyn,' Kennedy explained. 'By the time they turned round, he'd vanished.'

Nick shrugged. 'At least our suspicions are confirmed and we know he's there.'

Kennedy turned her tablet and showed them a GPS map. 'This is where Nesbitt was spotted. And there are two caravan parks here and here.' She pointed with her forefinger. 'It might narrow down where his brother is living.'

'Have we got a name for his brother?' Ruth asked.

Nick shook his head. 'Not at the moment.'

'Might be worth checking the council tax records or electoral roll for the surname Nesbitt,' Ruth said thinking out loud. 'My guess is that his brother won't be registered but if you can't find him, it's worth a try.'

Garrow came over, shirtsleeves now rolled up. 'I've pulled Darren Nesbitt's phone records. Digital Forensics are working on triangulating his phone and should have something within the hour.'

'Thanks, Jim,' Ruth said.

'Right,' Nick said decisively as he looked at Kennedy. 'Grab your coat. We're going to Prestatyn.'

'Ooh, lucky me,' Kennedy joked to Ruth sardonically as she and Nick walked away.

As Ruth headed back towards her office, she tried to get her head around what was now a very fast-moving investigation.

Her phone buzzed. It was a message from the North Wales Police Media Unit in St Asaph. They wanted to arrange for Ruth to do a national press conference at nine a.m. the following morning. Ashwin Choudary's murder was now the biggest news story in the country and trending across social media. There were also growing calls across social media for answers as to why the security in Bangor had been so inadequate. Ruth agreed with those concerns but she knew that as a representative of the North Wales Police and the Senior Investigating Officer – SIO – on the case, she would be the one having to field these questions later tomorrow morning. It wasn't something that she was looking forward to.

Taking a deep breath, Ruth felt the sudden urge for a cigarette. The stress of the day had really got to her.

Turning around, she looked at her watch. It was eight thirty p.m. The CID office was still a hive of activity. This was a high-profile murder case so the expectation was that the CID team would be working around the clock until those responsible were brought to justice. She'd be lucky to get four or five hours sleep a night for the foreseeable future.

Taking her phone, she sent Sarah a quick text.

> Going to be a late one. You okay? How's Daniel? Don't wait up (unless you really want to, ha ha!) Love you. R xxx

As Ruth went back into her office, she saw a woman in her mid-forties – smartly dressed, short blonde hair, attractive – was sitting on the small sofa at the far end working on a laptop.

Must be the DS that came with Rob.

'You must be DS Robinson?' Ruth said coming over and shaking her hand.

'Jane.'

'Jane. Right.'

'DI Hunter?' Jane asked with a smile.

Ruth detected a London accent. Or at least an estuary accent as they were now called.

'Ruth or boss,' she reassured her. 'Either one. You don't sound like you're from Manchester?'

'No,' Jane laughed. 'South London.'

Ruth's ears pricked up. South London was her birthplace. Her manor. 'Whereabouts?'

'Balham,' she said.

'You're joking?' Ruth snorted. 'I was born in Battersea. And I lived in Balham for years.'

Jane sat forward on the sofa. 'Right.' She gave a little chortle. 'Small world. Did you work in South London?'

'Did my probation at Lavender Hill nick.'

Jane gave her an incredulous look. 'So did I. When were you there?'

'Early Nineties,' Ruth replied.

'Ah, late Nineties for me,' she said.

'I was a DC in Peckham by then.'

Before they could continue, Rob walked in. 'Officers from the Witness Protection Unit will be here at seven a.m. tomorrow morning,' he explained. 'We'll need someone from the CPS to help thrash all this out with them.'

'I've got someone. Patricia Hoskins. Very sharp and no nonsense.' Then Ruth gestured out towards the doors to CID. 'Actually, I need a coffee and a cigarette. Okay if we walk and talk?'

'Of course,' Rob said gratefully. 'You've met Jane?'

Ruth nodded. 'Turns out we're from the same part of London and did our probation at the same nick.'

'Yeah, well you cockneys are a long way from home. You need to stick together,' he joked and then looked at Ruth. 'Coffee and fresh air sounds good.'

'Want to come with us?' Ruth asked Jane.

Jane gestured to her tablet. 'Waiting for some intel on British Action. Okay if I stay here? I couldn't find a free desk out there.'

'No problem,' Ruth reassured her. 'Make yourself at home.'

Ruth and Rob then strode across the CID office towards the double doors.

'I need to be careful hanging out with you,' he continued with a half-smile. 'I quit smoking five years ago but I still miss it.'

Rob opened the doors and gestured for Ruth to go first.

'Thank you,' she said as they went out and started to walk down the deserted corridor to the back staircase that led to the ground floor. 'I've tried to stop so many times. Bloody things.'

The police station was much quieter than during the day as there was only the night shift on.

'Witness Protection have a got a temporary safe house over by Bala Lake,' Rob explained as they walked down the stairs, shoes clattering noisily. 'Once we've had a meeting with them and the CPS tomorrow, Clarke and his family will be transferred across to Bala. They'll probably be there until after the trial. Then they'll be given a permanent new home.'

As they stepped out into the cold night air, Ruth lit a cigarette and stared across the darkened car park, her mind still racing. Everything was moving fast – too fast. Clarke's co-operation could blow the whole thing wide open, but if British Action got wind of it, they'd be coming for him, and anyone helping him. And with Nesbitt armed and desperate, hiding out in some static caravan on the North Wales coast, it wasn't just Clarke's family in danger – it was her team too.

Ruth exhaled slowly, the smoke curling in the still air. Somewhere out there, in the shadows, there were some very dangerous men who were going to make it their mission to ensure that Ray Clarke never made it to trial.

CHAPTER 14

It was nearly ten p.m. by the time Nick and Kennedy pulled into the Beachfront Holiday Caravan Park in Prestatyn. It was the first of the two caravan parks that Kennedy had identified as being close to where a uniformed patrol had spotted Nesbitt earlier. A trawl through Nesbitt's social media pages had revealed that his brother's name was Andy.

Getting out of the car, Nick glanced up into the clear night sky. The crescent moon was high above them and seemed to be tinged an icy blue at its curved edges. The rest of the black sky had a scattering of stars. Clouds were drifting in low from the sea now.

They were close to the North Wales coastline and the wind battered around them noisily. It came in gusts – restless and sharp – rattling the hedgerows and whispering through the gaps between the caravans.

The park itself was in virtual darkness. There were several rows of static caravans, most of which were unlit and presumably unoccupied. It was the middle of the week in October so that wasn't surprising. A faint smell of damp grass and diesel lingered in the air. Somewhere distant, a gull shrieked.

Nick scanned the area and spotted that there were three caravans with lights on. The nearest had an old Land Rover Defender parked outside. The other two caravans with lights were on the far side. They'd have to go down and take a look.

'Oi, what the hell do you think you're doing?' growled a man's voice.

Nick turned to see a bearded man in his sixties pointing a shotgun at them.

Oh, shit!

'Woah,' Kennedy said, holding her hands up at waist height. 'We're police officers. Can you put that gun down, please.'

The man frowned, looked them up and down and then lowered the gun.

'You got ID?' he asked suspiciously.

Nick and Kennedy pulled out their warrant cards. 'DS Evans and DC Kennedy, Llancastell CID.'

'Llancastell?' he snorted as he peered dubiously at the warrant cards. 'What the hell are you doing all the way over here?'

'We're looking for someone,' Kennedy replied. 'Darren Nesbitt? We understand that his brother Andy Nesbitt rents a static caravan somewhere around here.'

The man narrowed his eyes for a moment and then shook his head. 'Not in this park he doesn't.'

'I take it you're the owner,' Nick said.

He nodded. 'Yeah, that's right. We've had a series of break-ins. That's why I came up to see who you were. I reported it to your lot but they haven't done anything about it,' he sneered.

Nick gestured to the shotgun. 'Probably best that you don't go waving that thing around though. I assume you've got a licence for it?'

'Of course,' he snapped defensively. 'And if your lot won't do anything about it, I have to protect my park the best way I see fit.'

Nick exchanged a look with Kennedy. There seemed little point warning him that it only took a slip or an accident and he'd be spending the rest of his life in prison.

Kennedy pointed to where the lights were in the caravans on the far side. 'Okay, if we take a look anyway?'

The man shrugged. 'Be my guest. But he doesn't live here.'

'Thanks,' Nick said as they watched the man wander away.

'He was a charmer,' Kennedy joked.

'A charmer with a bloody shotgun,' Nick said dryly.

They walked along the dark row of caravans, their feet swooshing through the long grass. The wind swirled around and made low, eerie groaning sounds. A hanging gutter creaked rhythmically on one of the nearby units.

For the next ten minutes, Nick and Kennedy knocked on the doors of the three caravans, asking the residents if they knew Andy Nesbitt or if they'd seen the scooter or anything suspicious.

They drew a complete blank and made their way back to the car. Maybe they'd have more luck at the other caravan park, which was less than a mile south of where they were now.

CHAPTER 15

Ruth sat on the drive of her home in Bangor-on-Dee and a took a few moments. The day had been a whirlwind and she was exhausted. Part of her wanted to have a sneaky cigarette before she went inside. But if Sarah had waited up for her, she'd smell it and tell her off. Or worse. Give her that look of disappointment. Ruth could quickly chew some gum afterwards but she didn't think she had the energy to cover her tracks.

Opening the driver's door, she felt the sharp bite of the wind. The bells of the local church, St Dunawd's, rang to signal that it was eleven p.m. Ruth would catch a few hours' sleep before heading back to Llancastell CID.

She walked up the garden path, pushed the key into the front door and opened it, trying to keep the noise to a minimum so as not to wake up Daniel. The hall and living room lights were still on so she knew Sarah had waited up for her. Ruth got a little fizz of excitement at the thought of seeing Sarah and having a cuddle on the sofa. Maybe a big glass of wine too.

Hanging up her coat and kicking off her shoes, Ruth came into the living room and saw that Daniel was sitting on the sofa with Sarah.

Ruth raised an eyebrow. Something was up. 'Hi, guys.' Then she looked at Daniel. 'Couldn't you sleep?'

Daniel didn't reply but looked a little sheepish.

'Something happened at school today,' Sarah explained calmly. 'And Daniel is a little bit upset. So, I said he could wait up to see you.'

Ruth nodded, wondering what it was as she slumped down into the armchair. 'What's up then, buster?' she asked.

'Harvey and Elliot were teasing me,' Daniel mumbled.

'Teasing you?' Ruth said. 'Teasing you about what?'

Daniel shrugged but didn't respond.

Sarah sat forward. 'They were teasing him about the fact he's got two mums,' she said.

Ruth looked at Daniel who looked awkward. Although he wasn't yet a teenager, he was getting to that age where things like this would start to happen.

'Is that right?' Ruth asked.

Daniel nodded. 'They said you were "lezzies".'

Ruth frowned. 'Lezzies? I'm not sure that's even a word. I assume they were saying that we're lesbians. Sarah and I are gay. And we've talked about that with you lots, haven't we?'

Daniel looked down at the floor and nodded. 'But they were laughing at me.'

Sarah pulled a face. 'So, Daniel punched them. Mrs Matthews has suspended Daniel for a day and wants me to go in for a chat.'

'Ah,' Ruth nodded. Then she leaned forward. 'Daniel?' she said gently. Daniel took a moment then looked over at her. 'What Harvey and Elliot were saying and doing wasn't right. It was prejudiced. Do you remember we talked about that word?'

Daniel nodded but she wasn't convinced that he did remember. 'It means that someone doesn't like someone else based on their sexuality, their race, the colour of their skin, their religion. And it's not acceptable.'

Daniel gave a little nod to show that he understood.

'But it's not okay to hit someone because they are being prejudiced,' Ruth explained in a measured tone. 'As soon as you do that, you lose the argument. You come down to their level. Hurting someone is never the answer to anything. And if these boys continue to tease you, then Sarah and I can talk to Mrs Matthews. And if we have to, we can talk to their parents as well. But you mustn't do anything like this again, do you understand?'

Daniel nodded but he seemed to have tears in his eyes.

'Hey,' Ruth said sympathetically. 'Come here.'

Daniel got up, came over and Ruth wrapped her arms around him and hugged him tightly.

'You know how much Sarah and I love you,' she said in a virtual whisper. 'And I can understand why you wanted to stand up for us. But it's not the right thing to do. Okay?'

Daniel nodded and squeezed her tightly. 'Sorry,' he whispered.

Ruth looked over his shoulder at Sarah who gave her a reassuring smile.

CHAPTER 16

Nick and Kennedy got out of the car at the Prestatyn Beach Resort. A cold wind came in off the sea, carrying with it the tang of salt. As they peered into the darkness, they could see there were twice as many static caravans as the previous park. Long rows of them, stretched out under the faint orange glow of scattered security lights. But the good news was that there were about half a dozen caravans with their lights on, which increased their chances of finding either Darren or Andy Nesbitt.

Nick took out a powerful MagLite torch and gestured. 'Okay. Let's work our way down, shall we?'

'Yeah. Let's get this bastard,' Kennedy sneered, her voice low and tight.

As they moved along the gravelled path, their boots crunched rhythmically. A distant dog barked.

Nick glanced sideways at Kennedy. He wondered again how she was processing this. A case driven by racial hatred, a young man – Ashwin Choudary – gunned down by vile extremists. Kennedy was a person of colour. Did it hit closer to home for her? Was that edge in her voice righteous fury or something more personal?

He shoved the thought aside. Maybe it hadn't crossed her mind. Maybe that was just his own bias, his own discomfort. And anyway, this wasn't the time for introspection.

'Bingo!' Kennedy said, pointing up ahead.

A caravan stood about fifty yards away, every window lit. Vanilla light spilled out across the grass. But Kennedy wasn't pointing at the windows.

She was pointing to a black scooter parked directly outside.

Identical to the one Darren Nesbitt had been seen riding.

Got you, Nick thought as his pulse quickened.

As they got closer, Nick shone his torch onto the scooter. The licence plate matched. Darren Nesbitt was inside. Presumably with his brother Andy.

And if Darren was in there, chances were he had the firearm used in the Choudary killing.

Nick clicked off his torch.

'We'll take a quick look,' he whispered. 'Then we call for armed backup.'

Kennedy pulled a face. 'That could take ages,' she muttered.

'And going charging in there,' Nick said, 'could get us shot.'

Kennedy didn't reply, but he could feel her vibrating with frustration beside him.

They moved silently up the wooden staircase to the slatted deck surrounding the caravan. Each creak of the planks beneath their feet sounded amplified.

Nick crept to the front window, its flimsy curtains drawn. He moved his head slowly, peeking through the narrow gap at the edges.

A television flickered inside.

Two pairs of legs and feet – big, in Adidas trainers – protruded from a worn sofa.

But the angle didn't give him their faces.

He turned back to Kennedy.

'I can't see who that is,' he whispered.

She nodded tersely.

They edged along the decking. The shouts of a football commentary erupted from the caravan, muffled but clear enough – someone must've just scored.

Nick reached another window.

This one had no curtain. Inside was a cramped kitchen, yellowing counters cluttered with takeaway boxes and discarded lager cans.

Empty.

So far, two people.

But they needed more certainty before calling it in. The response would be completely different if there were two men versus a whole crew inside.

He ducked below the sill and gestured Kennedy to follow. They crouched low as they moved towards the back. The sound of the sea, faint but steady, filled the silence between their steps.

A small bedroom window revealed an unmade bed and a mess of clothes – no one inside.

They crept further until they reached a narrow window at the end of the caravan. A hallway beyond.

Then a door opened inside.

Before Nick could duck, a figure stepped into view.

Eyes locked.

Darren Nesbitt.

'Shit!' Nick hissed.

'What is it?' Kennedy whispered.

'Nesbitt. He's just spotted me.'

'Bollocks.'

Nick pivoted and sprinted back down the deck, torch back on.

'Sarge!' Kennedy called, chasing after him. 'Where are you going?'

Suddenly the caravan door burst open.

Darren Nesbitt exploded out, sprinting, then vaulted over the railing like a parkour athlete. His trainers hit the ground with a dull thud.

'Stop! Police!' Nick bellowed.

Nesbitt darted for his scooter.

'Sarge!' Kennedy shouted, her voice edged with panic.

Nick slowed his run. What if Nesbitt was armed?

Nesbitt slung a leg over the scooter, fumbling briefly – then his eyes found Nick.

He reached into his jacket and pulled out a black handgun.

Nick's heart thudded.

'Get down!' he roared at Kennedy, flinging himself to the ground.

A second of frozen silence.

Nick held his breath, waiting for gunshots.

Then the scooter screamed into life and tore down the gravel path, rear wheel kicking up stones.

Nick scrambled up, breath ragged. Kennedy met his eyes.

No way they were catching him now.

A figure appeared at the caravan doorway – a man in his late twenties, lanky, wide-eyed.

'Andy Nesbitt?' Nick asked, storming forward.

Andy raised his hands instinctively. 'I didn't know Daz had a gun. I swear.'

'Yeah, well you're under arrest,' Nick snapped, grabbing his arm. 'You can explain all that at the station.'

CHAPTER 17

It was just gone midnight when Nick pulled up outside his home. Over to the right, he noticed a parked car he didn't recognise. A smart-looking black Audi A4. It was sleek, freshly polished, the kind of car someone drove as a status symbol. There didn't appear to be anyone inside and there was no immediate reason for him to be suspicious.

Still, something about it didn't sit right.

Getting out of the car, Nick pulled up the collar on his coat against the chill of the night air. The wind had picked up, rustling the hedges and sending dry leaves skittering across the pavement. An owl was hooting somewhere in the distance, low and mournful, adding to his feeling of unease.

There was a sudden movement.

Out of the corner of his eye, Nick spotted something.

Spinning around, he braced himself.

Next door's cat jumped down from the bin and sprinted away.

Bloody hell. You little sod!

Nick blew out his cheeks, a puff of mist escaping into the air. He made his way to the front door and fished out his keys. It had been a long, stressful day and all he wanted now was to lie down next to Amanda and get some sleep.

He went inside. The house was lovely and warm, the radiators humming gently. There was a comforting smell of cooked food in the air – onions, maybe garlic – but he didn't have the energy to eat. His stomach felt tight, unsettled.

For a moment, Nick hesitated in the hallway. His old instinct – the one that used to take over when he was alone at night – gave him a fleeting image: pouring himself a triple vodka, maybe something neat and bitter.

Thank God those days were over.

He walked past the mirror and caught his own eyes. He looked tired. He remembered the last AA meeting he'd been to in Mold. Jimmy had sat beside him, gravel-voiced and straight-talking. Once a drug-dealing gangster from the West Midlands, Jimmy now ran a twelve-step rehab centre not far away. He'd been clean and sober for twelve years. During the meeting, Jimmy had shared his numbers – he'd helped nearly three thousand people get through that rehab. Only 1,200 were still alive.

Nick couldn't shake that statistic. Those were the odds and it was frightening.

Going into the living room, Nick noticed the small side lamp was still on. Amanda must have forgotten to turn it off when she went up to bed. Walking across the rug, his steps soft on the thick fibres, Nick reached for the switch, but something tugged at him a kind of habit, maybe paranoia. He moved back the curtain and looked outside.

The Audi was still parked up.

He squinted. The interior light was on now. Or seemed to be. A faint, ghostly glow lit the dashboard.

That can't be right.

There was still no one visibly inside. Maybe it was just the reflection from the streetlight. He told himself to let it go as it had been a draining day. He'd had a gun pointed at his head only two hours earlier. Then the long drive back. He needed rest, not more drama.

Nick shook off the unease. Out in the hallway, he kicked off his shoes, hung up his coat and jacket, and padded up the stairs, his socked feet making no sound.

He passed the bathroom, then reached Megan's room. Her door was open by a couple of inches. He pushed it wider and stepped inside, immediately enveloped by the soft pink light from her night light. She was asleep on her back, hands flung above her head in that trusting way only children had. A picture book rested against her shoulder, its pages curling.

With a warm smile, Nick moved gently across the room, eased the book away, and placed it on the shelf. He brushed a strand of hair from Megan's face. She stirred but didn't wake. That small, steady rhythm of her breathing filled him with something close to peace. The love he felt for her was vast. Protective.

Quietly, he pulled the door to and headed for the master bedroom. But he paused by the small hallway window overlooking the front of the house. Curiosity tugged at him again.

Moving the curtain aside, he peered down into the night.

The Audi hadn't gone.

But now there was a figure in the driver's seat.

Their face shadowed but unmistakably turned towards the house.

What the...?

Something twisted in his gut. A cold, creeping dread slithered up his spine. He turned, heart thudding, and moved swiftly along the landing, down the stairs two at a time, barely bothering to slip his shoes back on.

Who the hell is sitting outside our house like that? Watching?

Was it something to do with Keegan?

He reached the front door and wrenched it open, stepping out into the cold air. His breath was sharp in his throat as he marched down the path towards the iron gate, eyes fixed on the Audi.

Suddenly, the engine roared to life. They'd seen him.

Breaking into a run, Nick sprinted towards the car, trying to get a look at the driver. The headlights flared, momentarily blinding him.

The car pulled away at speed, tyres screeching a little.

All he managed to see was a man, head lowered, baseball cap on, dark hood pulled up. No plates visible from the front.

Nick whipped his phone from his pocket, but it was too later to get a photo of the car's registration.

'Nick?' called a voice.

He turned. Amanda was standing in the doorway, wrapped in her dressing gown, arms folded tightly against the cold. Her hair was messy, eyes wide with concern.

'What's going on?' she asked, her voice low.

'I don't know,' he said, making an effort to sound calm. He didn't want to frighten her, but Amanda wasn't daft. He didn't normally tear out of the house like this, shirt half-tucked, phone clutched in hand.

'Was that a car driving away?'

He nodded. 'It might be nothing.'

Amanda stepped aside as he came back in, closing the door behind him.

Then she turned, searching his face. 'You don't think it's nothing, do you?'

Nick met her gaze. 'I really don't know,' he said quietly. 'But I'll deal with it.'

She moved closer and he put his arms around her, holding her tightly.

'Do we need to be worried?' she whispered, breath warm against his chest.

'No,' he murmured, trying to sound firm. But the image of the watcher in the car wouldn't leave him. 'But just keep the doors and windows locked, until I check it out.'

Outside, the wind stirred again, and the night seemed to tighten around them.

CHAPTER 18

'Right, everyone,' Ruth said as she marched across the CID office and towards the scene boards to carry out the morning briefing. It was still pitch dark outside. The windows mirrored the fluorescent strip lights. 'Let's get up to speed on this.' She pointed to a photo. 'Our prime suspect is Darren Nesbitt. We know he's armed. Nick and Jade tracked him down to his brother's caravan in Prestatyn last night but he managed to escape. Any idea where he might have gone?'

'Andy Nesbitt is downstairs in a custody cell,' Nick explained. 'Jade and I are going to interview him this morning. We gave the caravan the once over, but there was nothing that might help us find him.'

'What's the brother like?' Ruth asked.

'Pretty scared,' Jade replied. 'He was babbling in the car on the way back. He says he didn't know that Darren had a gun or that he was involved in any kind of shooting.'

'Okay, let me know what he says,' Ruth said and then pointed to another photo. 'This is Raymond Clarke. He was Nesbitt's accomplice, although he also claims not to have known that Nesbitt had a gun or had any intention of shooting Choudary. He's agreed to co-operate fully with this investigation. We have officers from the Witness Protection Unit coming here today and they'll thrash out the details with the CPS.'

Garrow looked over. 'Is Clarke willing to testify against the leaders of British Action?'

'He says that he is,' Ruth said. 'And his testimony that they ordered the assassination of Ashwin Choudary will be a significant step in getting these men'—Ruth pointed to the photos of the men who lead British Action—'convicted of conspiracy to murder. And, as we all know, that can carry a life sentence. But we're going to need more evidence than Clarke's testimony to get a conviction. Where are we at with Clarke's phone records?'

Garrow looked over. 'I've got several numbers calling Clarke's phone on a regular basis in the two weeks before the shooting. I've done a check with a phone provider but turns out that they're all burners.'

'Burners' meant a pay-as-you-go mobile phone which were very hard to track or trace, and therefore perfect for keeping calls and texts private. Criminals often only used them for short periods of time before destroying them and buying another so as to reduce the chances of being traced even more.

'Any chance we can get surveillance on them?' Kennedy asked.

'I'll see what Counter Terrorism have got,' Ruth replied. Her voice was tight, jaw clenched. 'But I want us to liaise with Counter Terrorism and build a case against these scumbags,' she said, pointing to the photos again. 'Right, let's get cracking. Thank you, everyone.'

CHAPTER 19

Ruth walked along the ground floor of Llancastell nick and came to the main meeting room. The corridor smelled faintly of damp wool and stale coffee. Overhead, the lights buzzed with a low hum. She paused at the door, gathered her thoughts, then pushed it open.

As she went in, she saw that Rob was sitting over on the far side. His posture was rigid, and he gave her a tight nod. Next to him were two officers from the Witness Protection Unit. Detective Constable Bhutto, an Asian woman in her thirties with a pretty face and wearing a smart navy trouser suit, and Detective Inspector Callaghan, a silver-haired man in his fifties who wore a casual jacket with a navy sweater underneath. Callaghan looked like he'd walked out of an old Seventies crime drama and never quite left the role.

To Ruth's right was Patricia Hoskins – forties, smart, blonde, glasses – a lawyer from the North Wales Crown Prosecution. Ruth had worked with Hoskins before. She was sharp as a whip, didn't suffer fools, but Ruth liked her no-nonsense honesty. She was also one of the few people Ruth trusted not to underestimate her.

Ruth came over to the oval table as everyone introduced themselves and shook hands. Then she sat down. As SIO, it was her job to take the lead in this meeting, though the weight of it sat heavily on her shoulders today. There seemed to be so many moving pieces. Plus the focus of the UK's media was on how North Wales Police were handling Ashwin Choudary's murder and the subsequent fallout.

'Patricia,' Ruth said, looking across the table. Hoskins was always 'Patricia' – never 'Pat', never 'Trish'. Ruth remembered a young DC calling her 'Trish' once and Hoskins putting her promptly in her place.

'How did it go with Clarke this morning?' Ruth asked, kicking things off.

Hoskins had already met with Raymond Clarke and the duty solicitor to explain to Clarke what would be required of him if he and his family were going to be taken into Witness Protection.

Hoskins took a moment, then said, 'He didn't seem keen on testifying in court and coming face to face with the leaders of British Action. But I made it very clear that unless he did that, he and his family were on their own.'

Ruth nodded. She felt a flicker of unease. 'I'm hoping that he can provide us with concrete evidence that they organised for Clarke and Nesbitt to attend the event in Bangor yesterday and assassinate Ashwin Choudary.'

Rob leaned forward over the table. 'It would certainly be a lot easier if Clarke had known that Nesbitt had a gun and was planning to shoot Ashwin Choudary.'

'What makes you think he didn't?' DI Callaghan asked in a slightly offhand tone.

Ruth glanced over at him. She wasn't one for snap judgements but he was already getting up her nose.

'I think mine and Ruth's instinct was that he didn't,' Rob admitted, sounding a tad defensive. 'But conspiracy would be much easier to prove if Clarke had received a direct order from them.'

Hoskins pushed her glasses up the bridge of her nose. 'Clarke admitted that the assassination of Ashwin Choudary had been discussed on several occasions during British Action meetings. Personally, I think he's lying to save his own skin.'

'Might be worth re-interviewing him again and really push him to see what he knows,' DI Callaghan suggested with a slightly pompous tone. 'Especially now he's got immunity from prosecution.' He looked at Hoskins. 'It would make your job at trial a lot easier.'

Ruth bristled. DI Callaghan was overstepping the mark a little. It was her call whether or not to pressure Clarke. She held his gaze just a moment longer than was necessary – long enough to remind him she wasn't to be managed – then looked away.

There were a few seconds of silence.

Outside, the drizzle began again, soft at first but with the promise of something more relentless. Rain always brought a strange electricity to Llancastell nick.

'Clarke is fragile,' Ruth said carefully. 'If we push too hard now, he could fold completely. He's no zealot – he's terrified.'

She remembered the tremble in Clarke's voice when he'd spoken about Bangor. The fear had been real. Not just fear of prison – but of what might follow. Ruth had seen it before. That particular brand of dread didn't come from guilt. It came from men who knew they were being hunted.

Rob nodded, his face drawn. 'He's got two teenage kids, Ruth. He's not built for this.'

Hoskins leaned forward, voice low. 'Then let's hope fear of British Action outweighs his fear of being in the dock.'

CHAPTER 20

Inside Interview Room 1, Andy Nesbitt was dressed in a grey sweatshirt and trackies. His blond hair was messy and his eyes moved nervously around the room.

Nick pulled in his chair and looked over at Nesbitt. His foot was tapping nervously on the floor. The tension in the room was already ratcheting up.

Nick looked at Kennedy and then at the duty solicitor to confirm they were ready to start. He leaned over and pressed the red button on the digital recording equipment. There was a long, loud electronic beep.

'Interview conducted with Andrew Nesbitt, Interview Room 1, Llancastell Police Station. Present are Detective Constable Jade Kennedy, duty solicitor Keith Jones and myself, Detective Sergeant Nick Evans. Time is'—he glanced at his tablet—'eleven twenty-three a.m.'

Nick raised his eyebrow and looked over. 'Andy?'

Andy looked up and blinked nervously.

'I'm just going to remind you that you are under arrest for aiding and abetting a fugitive,' Nick said sternly. 'The maximum sentence for this offence is ten years in prison.'

The colour visibly drained from Andy's face. It clearly wasn't something that he'd discussed with his duty solicitor. 'And given that your brother Darren is wanted in connection with a murder,' Nick continued, 'I would suggest that a maximum sentence is very likely.'

'But I didn't know he was wanted for that,' Andy blurted out anxiously.

Nick glanced at Kennedy. Andy clearly wasn't going to go 'no comment' for the interview which was surprising.

Kennedy leaned forward. 'When did Darren arrive at your caravan, Andy?'

'Yesterday afternoon,' he replied.

'And when was the last time you'd seen him before that?' she asked.

'Not for a few months,' he admitted.

'Were you surprised to see him?' Kennedy continued.

Andy took a few seconds. 'A bit,' he shrugged.

'Why was that?' Kennedy asked.

Andy then shrugged again but there was definitely something he wasn't telling them.

Nick scratched at his beard and then narrowed his eyes. 'What was your relationship like with your brother, Andy?'

Andy fidgeted nervously. 'It was all right,' he mumbled unconvincingly.

Nick raised an eyebrow quizzically. 'Had you fallen out or argued recently?'

Andy gave a slight nod of his head.

'For the purposes of the recording,' Nick said, 'the suspect has nodded his head.'

Silence.

'What had you fallen out about?' Nick asked, wondering if it had anything to do with Darren Nesbitt's extreme political views.

Andy didn't look like he wanted to answer.

Kennedy frowned. 'Andy, did you know that Darren was a member of British Action?'

Andy nodded again and then bit at the nails on his right hand. 'Yes,' he said under his breath.

'Is that what you argued with Darren about?' Kennedy asked.

Andy nodded again and visibly took a breath. 'Yeah.'

'Didn't you approve of Darren being a member of British Action?' Kennedy said.

Andy shook his head. 'No.'

Nick tapped at his tablet, found a photo of Ashwin Choudary and then turned to show Andy. 'Do you know who this man is, Andy?'

'I didn't.' Andy scratched his forehead nervously. 'But then I saw the news.'

'Did Darren say anything about this man when he was with you?' Nick said.

Andy leaned forward on his seat and bit at his nails again. 'Yeah. He said he was glad that someone had shot him dead.'

'But he didn't say that he'd had anything to do with Ashwin Choudary's murder?' Nick asked.

'Not at first,' Andy explained. 'Then he said he knew who'd done it.'

'Did he tell you how he knew who had killed Ashwin Choudary?'

'He didn't need to.' Andy shrugged. 'I knew he meant his mates from British Action.'

'And how did that make you feel?' Nick said.

Andy pulled a face. 'It was horrible.'

'You don't share your brother's extreme political views?' Kennedy asked.

'No,' Andy replied adamantly. 'No way. We had enough of all that shit when we were kids.'

Nick frowned. 'Your father held those kinds of views then?'

Andy nodded. 'Yeah, he was a racist prick. Went on marches.' Andy took a breath. 'I saw him and his mates once beat up a Pakistani man for no reason other than the colour of his skin. It made me feel sick. I swore that I'd never be like that.'

Nick watched him closely. The room had changed. The defensive tension had shifted, replaced with something raw, ugly, and much older than yesterday's arrest.

'But Darren didn't feel like that?' Kennedy asked.

'No. I suppose he wanted our father's approval,' Andy admitted. 'Darren started to go to political meetings with him when he was a teenager. And they'd go to the football and get into fights with other fans.'

'But you didn't?'

'No. I wasn't interested,' Andy said. Talking about his childhood had clearly made him angry. 'They were bloody idiots.'

'What did they think about you not going with them?' Kennedy said.

'They said I was a gay pussy.' Andy sighed. 'I left home at sixteen. My dad found out that I'd been seeing a mixed-race girl at school so he beat me up and spat on me.'

Jesus, Nick thought to himself as Kennedy gave him a look. He now felt sorry for Andy and what he'd been through. It certainly didn't sound as if he'd aided or abetted his brother.

Andy slouched a little in his chair.

The silence hung for a moment, long and deliberate.

'Do you know where Darren might have gone?' Nick asked.

Andy nodded. 'I've got a pretty good idea.'

'You think he will have gone to your father's home?' Kennedy said to clarify.

'Yeah,' Andy said.

Nick looked at him. 'Can you give us the address?'

Andy nodded slowly.

The room fell silent except for the whir of the air vent.

'Thank you, Andy,' Nick said in a quiet, genuine tone. He slid a piece of A4 paper and a pen over to Andy who started to write.

Nick exchanged a look with Kennedy, her face still taut.

CHAPTER 21

By the time Ruth had sat down to conduct the morning North Wales Police press conference, she was already aware that someone had leaked to the press that there had been several death threats against Ashwin Choudary by British Action and other far-right extremists. Choudary's outspoken views on immigration, as well as the growth of right-wing politics in the UK, had made him an obvious target.

The conference room smelled faintly of stale coffee and old carpet cleaner. The low murmur of journalists settling in their seats added to Ruth's underlying anxiety.

The question that was being asked both in the traditional media, as well as online, was that if there had been death threats, why had Ashwin Choudary's security been so inadequate in Bangor? As far as Ruth knew, there had only been two uniformed officers present in the hall when Choudary had given his speech. There had been no searches conducted on those attending and no officers with any meaningful intel watching those attending for right-wing extremists. Clarke and Nesbitt both had distinctive tattoos for starters, yet no one had spotted them.

It gnawed at her how easily Nesbitt and Clarke had slipped through the net.

There was a tweet on Twitter:

> **BBC Wales@BBCWales Breaking News**
>
> Sources claim that murdered MP Ashwin Choudary had received death threats in the months leading up to his assassination. Those death threats are alleged to have come from the far-right terror group British Action. A spokesperson for North Wales Police refused to comment on allegations that the security surrounding Ashwin Choudary's appearance at Bangor's Festival of Words was wholly inadequate.

Ruth's heart sank as she looked out at the assembled reporters. She had never liked holding press conferences at the best of times. But today, she was going to be grilled about the death threats and the lack of security.

Her blouse itched at the collar, and her pulse thudded at her temples. This was going to be difficult.

Glancing up, she saw Kerry Mahoney arriving and heading towards the chair next to her. Mahoney had previously been the Chief Corporate Communications Officer for North Wales Police based at the main press office in Colwyn Bay. However, as far as Ruth knew, Mahoney had retired, which was a relief. Mahoney had been nothing but arrogant and patronising in every encounter that Ruth had ever had with her.

Ruth gave her a forced smile. 'Hello, Kerry,' Ruth said quietly. 'I thought you'd taken early retirement.'

'So did I,' Mahoney said as she moved in her seat to get comfortable. 'But the media department has struggled to find a suitable replacement since I left. They begged me to come back on a part-time basis, so here I am. I guess being irreplaceable is one of the downsides of being good at your job,' she added without any modicum of humility.

'I guess,' Ruth said with another forced smile.

Oh, get over yourself, you snotty cow, Ruth thought to herself.

'Right, we'd better get on,' Mahoney said, gesturing out to the assembled journalists and camera crew.

On the table in front of them was a row of microphones.

Ruth cleared her throat. 'Good morning, I'm Detective Inspector Ruth Hunter of North Wales Police, and I am the Senior Investigating Officer in the murder of Ashwin Choudary, the MP for the Bangor Aberconwy constituency. Beside me is Kerry Mahoney, our Chief Corporate Communications Officer. This press conference is to update you on the case and to appeal to the public for any information regarding Mr Choudary's murder on Monday at an event at Penrhyn Hall. We believe that Mr Choudary was shot and killed at close range by this man.' Ruth turned and pointed to a photo behind her. 'Darren Nesbitt, a member of the proscribed far-right terrorist group, British Action. Darren Nesbitt is currently on the run, and we would like to hear from anyone who knows where he is or thinks that they have seen him recently. However, I would urge members of the public not to approach this man as he is armed and dangerous. If you do have information'—Ruth pointed to a sign behind her on the wall—'please call one of these hotline numbers. You can remain anonymous. I have a few minutes to take some questions.'

'Can you confirm that there had been several death threats against Ashwin Choudary from members of British Action?' asked a reporter from the front row.

Here we go! Ruth thought.

'I'm afraid that's not information that I have at this precise moment. However, the Independent Office for Police Conduct will be doing a thorough investigation surrounding the terrible events on Monday,' Ruth said, but she knew that this wasn't going to satisfy the reporters in the room. She heard a few mumbles and grumbles.

'I have a source that claims there were only two police officers on duty at the event on Monday,' another journalist said sternly. 'If Ashwin Choudary's life was in serious danger, how do you explain this complete lack of security at a public event?'

'I can only reiterate what I've already told you. There will be a full investigation into the events on Monday. If there were lapses in security, then those responsible will be held to account.'

The reporter shook his head. 'That's not going to be of much comfort to Ashwin Choudary's wife and children, is it?' he snapped.

Another reporter stood up to Ruth's right. 'You've come here to talk to the media, but you're refusing to answer one of the key questions that everyone here wants to know. Instead, you're fobbing us off, as always, with an IOPC investigation that will take months, if not years, to publish its findings. Some of those responsible for what happened on Monday will have taken early retirement, no doubt. And, as always, no one will be held accountable.'

There were murmurs of agreement from some of the other journalists in the room.

Ruth took a nervous swallow as the pressure grew.

Mahoney leaned over to her microphone. 'Right, thank you, everyone. No more questions.'

Ruth gave her a begrudging nod of thanks as she stood and gathered up her files. She noticed Mahoney giving her a slightly conceited look. She had spotted that Ruth was a bit rattled, and she was judging her.

Right, you can fuck off for starters, Ruth thought as she brushed past Mahoney and headed out. *And I'm definitely going to need a ciggie and a coffee before I make the drive to Bala Lake.*

CHAPTER 22

'So, what made you want to become a copper?' Rob asked Ruth as they sped out of Corwen, heading across the undulating backbone of Snowdonia towards Bala.

They'd been on the road for about forty-five minutes, and Ruth was relishing the rare luxury of being behind the wheel. She always insisted on Nick driving, mainly so she could smoke. She also knew that Nick loved being behind the wheel. It was probably something to do with his own residual belief that he was Lewis Hamilton trapped in a Vauxhall Astra.

They were deep into Snowdonia now. The land had shifted around them, grown taller, more muscular. Jagged ridgelines rose, their peaks mist-shrouded. Llyn Celyn lay still to the west, a mirror of sky and stone. On either side of the road, drystone walls crumbled into heather, and sheep grazed with indifference.

Ruth always felt small in places like this. But not in a bad way. It was a kind of cleansing. A reminder that whatever chaos she dealt with day to day – murders, missing kids, racist paramilitaries – none of it mattered to the mountains.

She glanced in the rear view mirror. The patrol car behind kept a respectful distance. Clarke sat between the uniforms, head bowed under a cap and sunglasses. A makeshift disguise.

'Why did I become a copper?' she said aloud, giving herself a second to think. 'Because of my dad, I guess.'

'He was a copper?'

She let out a dry laugh. 'Hardly. He was a crook. Petty South London thief. Used to say things like "I'm a businessman" while flogging knock-off TVs from the back of a van. Dodgy as hell.'

Rob looked sideways. 'And that made you want to join the police?'

'Exactly that. I got sick of watching him lie and cheat his way through life. He never gave a toss about me or my brother. One year, he gave my brother a bike for Christmas. Dark blue Chopper.'

'Classic,' Rob said. 'My brothers had them.'

'Turned out it was stolen. A man and his son stopped him in the street, turned it over, spotted a JET sticker. Said it'd been taken in Balham. Took it back on the spot. My brother cried all the way home. Dad promised he'd get him another. Never did.'

The lake appeared again as they crested the hill. Ruth squinted into the windscreen as light flickered across the water's surface.

'So, yeah,' she said. 'I wanted to be the opposite of him. Do something useful and make a difference. I know it sounds like a cheesy cliché.'

'Doesn't sound cheesy at all,' Rob replied, then after a pause: 'I joined because of my dad too. He was in the job. It felt inevitable, really.'

'No regrets?' she asked.

'Sometimes. It's not the job it used to be,' he admitted.

'Thank God,' she said, too fast.

Rob looked at her. 'You think so?' He sounded surprised which was a red flag.

She exhaled. She'd hoped to avoid this. Not today.

'You were a white male in the Nineties, Rob. I imagine it was a very different job for you,' she said, trying not to sound frustrated or patronising.

'Maybe. I suppose so,' he said but it was half-hearted. 'But these days it's all so bloody "woke". Can't say anything. Can't do anything. It's box-ticking and bureaucracy. And don't get me started on recruitment and positive discrimination. Jesus.'

Ruth held up a hand, getting sucked in. 'You mean accountability and representation?'

He gave her a glance. Defensive. Wary. 'I've seen good officers passed over. Replaced by candidates who weren't ready. Not because they were better – but because they ticked the diversity box. We're not supposed to say that, but it's happening.'

'Maybe they were better in ways you couldn't see,' Ruth said quietly. 'Because the old system didn't give people like them a chance in the first place.'

She could feel her heartbeat rise, but her voice stayed calm. This was the part that always got her. When good people, decent officers, revealed that they didn't fully understand how broken the system had been – and still was.

She glanced at him again. Did she want to fight this out now?

No. She stored it. Like evidence. It would be there when and if she needed it.

There was an awkward few seconds of silence as their previous conversation hung in the air.

'Turning's up here,' Rob said eventually, pointing to a gravel track.

They were both relieved to be back in the present.

The farmhouse appeared ahead. It had stone walls and was detached and very remote. Trees lined the lower fields, and below that, Bala Lake shimmered silver and pale blue under the sinking sun.

'Wow. Hell of a spot,' Rob said. 'Beats Manchester hands down.'

'It's called Llyn Tegid,' Ruth said.

'What is?'

'The lake. Welsh for Bala Lake. And the biggest lake in Snowdonia National Park. Or Eryri as we now call it.'

Rob raised an amused eyebrow. 'You're going native.'

'I'm starting to,' she admitted with a smile. 'My DS tells me this stuff in the car. I've started remembering it.'

They pulled in, the tyres crunching on gravel. Then they got out.

Ruth gave a little stretch of her arms and looked at the view.

The car stopped behind them. One of the uniforms got out stiffly and went to the back door.

'Out we get,' he said to Clarke.

Rob scrolled his phone. 'Entry code's in the briefing notes. Should be keys inside. MI6 used this place for a while when they kept terror suspects here. So, it's basically Fort Knox. Motion sensors, reinforced doors, infrared cameras.'

Ruth grabbed her overnight holdall. She'd be staying until Witness Protection officers arrived. It could be hours and it was more likely to be tomorrow.

She pulled out a cigarette, cupped her hand and lit it. 'I'll be in shortly.'

As Clarke passed her, his eyes flicked to the packet.

She held it out. 'Want one?'

He hesitated. 'Really?'

'Go on.'

He took one. She lit it for him, noticing the slight tremor in his hands.

'Come on, move it,' the uniformed officer snapped.

Ruth held his gaze. 'He's fine. I can take it from here, Constable.'

The officer gave a grunt and walked off back towards the car, muttering.

Clarke took a drag and looked out at the lake. 'It's beautiful here,' he said. 'I promised the kids we'd do a trip to Wales one day. Snowdonia. Or the coast. But work got busy. Then everything else… happened.'

Bala Lake stretched out before them, long and dark and calm. The light shimmered across its surface in ripples. A pair of ducks cut through the water near the reeds. Beyond, the slopes of the mountains rolled up into the sky, dusky and quiet, as if watching over the surrounding land.

Ruth let her eyes rest on it. There was something ancient about the place – serene and unbothered. For thousands of years, it had seen people come and go, lies told, secrets buried, all without blinking.

'You ever been before?' she asked.

He shook his head. 'Never left Stoke, really. Never thought I needed to. Until now.'

Ruth watched him. Beneath the bravado, there was something smaller. Something worn thin. Men like Clarke weren't masterminds. They were cannon fodder. The kind British Action knew how to use.

'They said they'd fix things,' Clarke said. 'Said the government was corrupt, that we were losing our identity. Said I'd be part of a movement. Something real.'

Ruth raised an eyebrow. 'What did they want in return?'

He shrugged. 'I'm not sure. But I thought I was helping. Thought I was fighting back.' He let out a bitter laugh. 'I thought I was doing it for my kids.' Clarke looked down at the cigarette, already half-burned. 'I thought I was doing something that mattered.'

'You still can,' Ruth said. 'Help us now, and you might still make something of this.'

Clarke frowned. He looked lost. 'You reckon that's possible?'

Ruth didn't answer right away. A breeze swept up from the valley, rustling through the trees.

'I think people get second chances,' she said finally. 'But not forever.'

They stood in silence for a moment longer.

'I owe to it Sheila too,' Clarke said in a low tone. 'We only got married two years ago. And she's been so good with Chelsie and Alfie.' Clarke blew out a long plume of smoke with a sigh. 'And now all this…'

Ruth looked at him. 'All you can do from now is the next right thing.'

Clarke tapped the ash from his cigarette. He was deep in thought.

'I should go in,' he said eventually, and stubbed out the cigarette on a stone.

Ruth nodded.

He turned, walked up the path towards the house, shoulders hunched a little.

Ruth stayed where she was, watching the lake catch the light and taking a final drag on her cigarette.

CHAPTER 23

Nick and Kennedy had travelled across the border to Market Drayton, heading to the address that Andy Nesbitt had given them for his father, Ian. Market Drayton was a town balanced on the edge of the Cheshire and Staffordshire borders. Nick knew it. He'd been there in his drinking days.

Kennedy looked up as they passed the crooked, slightly rusted sign that welcomed them to the town:

> Welcome to Market Drayton – Home of Gingerbread.
> Twinned with Pézenas and Arlon

'Well, I never knew that,' Kennedy said dryly, raising a single brow.

'The home of gingerbread?' Nick smiled.

'Apparently.'

'Yep. Centre of the UK's gingerbread industry since the 1800s.' His tone was light and playful.

Kennedy nodded, bemused. 'Good to know.'

'They used to have a cracking beer festival here,' Nick said, tapping at the satnav, eyes flicking between the screen and the road as he followed the route to Ian Nesbitt's house. 'Came a few times with some mates. We camped over. It got very messy.'

'You ever miss it?' Kennedy asked, glancing at him. Her tone was casual, but Nick could feel the undertone. A gentle probing. She was good at that.

'Drinking?' he clarified.

She nodded. 'Yeah.'

'Oh, no,' Nick said, shaking his head. 'Not one bit. And if I did miss it, well I wouldn't be able to stay sober.'

Kennedy frowned. 'How do you mean?'

'In AA we call it "white-knuckling it",' Nick explained, eyes narrowing as he made a left turn onto a narrow residential street. 'If you carry on missing alcohol, craving it, wishing you could drink. Eventually your willpower just runs out. You give in. Press the "fuck it" button...'

Kennedy gave a short laugh. 'The "fuck it" button? I like that.'

'And once it's pressed,' Nick continued, voice lower now, 'you drink again. Because it's too hard to stop. You've got to surrender. Completely.'

'Surrender?' Kennedy echoed, confused.

'If I have one drink, I want another. And another. My head tells me to keep drinking until I pass out. I've got no off switch. No moderation. So, I surrender. I have to accept that alcohol's more powerful than I am. And eventually, after a while, with that mindset, you are no longer interested in alcohol. That feeling, craving, just goes away.'

He paused.

Kennedy was quiet for a moment. 'That craving really just... goes?'

Nick nodded. 'Eventually. If you do the work, go to meetings, get honest. But sometimes...' He paused. 'I'll drive past a pub and see some bloke with a cold pint. And my brain whispers, *Wouldn't that be nice?* But I know I could never just sit and have one pint.'

'Why not?' Kennedy asked, genuinely trying to understand.

'I never saw the point of one or two,' Nick said, turning to look at her. 'I drank to get smashed. So, I'd have that pint, then sneak in a couple of double JDs. Four, five pints. Buy more booze on the way home. Blackout. Wake up soaked in my own piss, searching the kitchen for more. That's how it always went.'

Kennedy exhaled through pursed lips as Nick pulled the car to a halt. 'You describe it so vividly. It sounds... horrendous.'

'It is,' Nick said flatly. 'And that's why I work hard never to go back.'

Kennedy nodded. 'Good for you.' She sounded genuinely pleased for him.

Nick gave a slight shrug and nodded towards the house they were now parked outside. 'Right, shall we?'

'Carefully does it though, Sarge,' Kennedy murmured.

Ian Nesbitt's house looked tired and shabby. The paint flaked from the window frames like sunburned skin. Ivy had started to creep up the brickwork. The gutters sagged under the weight of soil and weeds.

On the cracked driveway sat a battered white Transit van, *Nesbitt Plumbers* printed on the side in faded lettering. A large St George's Cross adorned the back window, next to a handwritten mobile number in permanent marker.

'Looks like he's at home,' Nick said, pointing at the van.

'No sign of any scooter,' Kennedy noted, scanning the property as they stepped from the car.

Nick moved to the right of the house, peering cautiously down the side alley. Just bins. No movement. Still, his pulse ticked faster. Darren Nesbitt was armed and volatile. They'd be fools to underestimate him or the danger that he posed.

Reaching the porch, Nick noticed the doorstep was thick with dried mud. A small plastic bag sat to one side, overflowing with crushed beer cans. The stale tang of lager hung in the air, mixing with the scent of wet dogs.

'Here we go,' he muttered, his heart thudding as he rapped heavily on the door.

Inside, barking erupted. Then silence.

A moment later, the door creaked open. A gaunt man in his sixties stared out at them. He had a shaved head and narrow eyes. His white vest was stained, clinging to a concave chest. Camouflage shorts hung low on his hips.

'Oh, great,' he said with a theatrical groan. 'I knew it wouldn't be long before you lot came banging on my bloody door. Well, he's not here.'

'Ian Nesbitt?' Nick asked in a tone designed to show that he was taking charge.

The man snorted a laugh. 'Yeah.'

'We're looking for your son, Darren,' Kennedy said, her voice firm.

Ian gave them a long, contemptuous look. 'Are you two thick or something? I just told you. He ain't here.' He stepped back and swept his arm inside. 'Come in, have a nose about if you don't believe me.'

Nick exchanged a surprised glance with Kennedy. That wasn't expected. He'd assumed that there would have been aggressive demands for a search warrant.

'My son's not a moron. He knew you'd check here,' Ian muttered as they stepped inside. The hallway was musty. Wallpaper peeled at the corners. The carpet was gritty underfoot.

'You've spoken to him recently?' Nick asked, scanning the room.

'Nah,' Ian grunted but it was unconvincing. He was definitely lying to them.

Then his eyes flicked to Kennedy and a sneer curled his lip. 'Dear, oh dear. They really will let anyone in the force these days. Talk about scraping the bloody barrel.'

Nick's fists clenched. He wanted to deck the man. Just one swift, satisfying punch to the jaw. But he forced himself to breathe. Kennedy gave Nick a small nod – she was fine. She wouldn't give Nesbitt the satisfaction.

'Okay if we look around?' Nick said evenly, ignoring him.

'Be my guest.' Nesbitt smirked. 'Would offer you tea and biscuits'—he looked at Kennedy again—'or would *you* prefer a banana?'

Nick's temper snapped. He stepped forward, into Nesbitt's personal space, until their faces were inches apart.

'Listen, you sad little man,' he said, voice low and hard. 'Sit down and shut up. Say one more thing, and I'll bring a unit in here to tear this place apart. Then I'll arrest you, bounce you around a cell and let every copper in the West Midlands know you're helping us with our inquiries. Publicly.'

Nesbitt stared at him. But there was no fear. Just that infuriating smirk. Then, without a word, he turned and walked into the front room, laughing to himself.

Kennedy exhaled. 'Thanks, Sarge,' she whispered.

'No problem.' Nick's hands were still clenched tight. He forced them open. 'Let's have a look around.'

They moved from room to room.

The place was a mess – not quite squalid, but close. Newspapers from last year lay under a broken table. A crusted saucepan sat in the sink, fossilised spaghetti clinging to its rim.

Ten minutes passed. But there was no sign of Darren. No fresh clothing, no used mugs or second toothbrush. No sense that another person had recently been here.

But Nick didn't feel at ease.

Entering the back bedroom, Nick saw a huge St George's Cross up on the wall. Printed underneath was:

ENGLAND ON TOUR – STOKE CTY NAUGHTY 40

Nick gave a withering sigh and crouched down, looking beneath the bed. Dust, an old shoe, and a half-empty bottle of Bell's.

Then something caught his eye. A coffee mug sitting on the carpet beside the bed.

Looking inside, he saw that the inch of coffee inside was still liquid. It was relatively new.

He stood and moved to the chest of drawers. Opened one. It was empty. The next – also empty. Inside the third was a pack of razors, a comb, but nothing else. A drawer that had recently been cleared.

He turned to Kennedy. 'I think Darren has been here,' he said. 'I'd bet money on it.'

But Kennedy didn't answer him. She was distracted.

'Everything all right?' Nick asked.

Kennedy pulled back the yellowing net curtain at the window.

'There's a woman across the road looking out of her window,' Kennedy explained with a nod of her head. 'I think we should go and have a chat, see if she's seen anything.'

CHAPTER 24

Ruth took the boiling kettle from its stand and poured the water into four mugs that all had tea bags in. She was standing in the kitchen of the safe house. Sitting at the table was Clarke's wife, Sheila. She was in her forties, too much make-up, collagen lips, and wore a hoodie and jeans. Her face was red and puffy from where she'd been crying. Ruth didn't blame her. Her whole life had been turned upside down in the past few days.

Ruth looked over and saw Sheila gazing blankly out of the window. She looked shellshocked by what had happened. Sheila had arrived with the two teenage step-children – Alfie and Chelsie – about half an hour ago. They'd brought suitcases which Alfie had taken upstairs. Chelsie seemed very angry and didn't understand why she couldn't have her phone.

Ruth stirred the tea, added milk and then handed the mug of tea to Sheila.

'Ta,' she whispered in her Brummie accent.

Ruth then delivered the other two mugs to Clarke and Rob who were in the living room. Clarke was watching TV and Rob was on his tablet working. Jane had just arrived and was unpacking her stuff upstairs.

Ruth then returned to the kitchen, took her own mug of tea and sat down opposite Sheila who gave her a forced smile.

'I didn't know Ray was doing any of this, you know?' she explained.

Ruth frowned. 'You must have had some idea?'

Sheila sighed, then sipped her tea and shrugged. 'I knew he had some mates. And I knew he'd been on a couple of marches.' Then she shook her head in disbelief. 'But what happened to that poor man in Bangor. I can't believe that Ray was mixed up in that. He's just not like that.'

Ruth thought for a second and then said, 'But you must have known about Ray's political views?'

'Not really,' Sheila admitted. 'We don't really talk about politics. I know he hates immigrants, but most people do where we live. It's normal.'

'You didn't know he was going to Bangor with Darren Nesbitt?' Ruth asked.

'No,' Sheila said emphatically. 'If I'd known that Ray was going anywhere with Darren, I would have stopped him.'

Ruth raised an eyebrow. 'Why's that?'

'Darren is a headcase,' Sheila snorted, jabbing her forefinger into her temple to emphasise the point. 'The last time Ray was out with Darren, he came back with a black eye. Some lefty do-gooder punched him when they were demonstrating about putting immigrants in a local hotel.' Sheila took a breath and looked upset. 'I kept telling him not to get himself mixed up in any of it but he wouldn't listen to me. And now this has happened.' Her eyes filled with tears.

Ruth reached into her pocket, pulled out a small packet of tissues and handed it to her. 'Here you go,' she said gently.

'Ta,' Sheila said as she took one out and dabbed at her eyes. 'My bloody mascara is running. I'm gonna look like a panda.'

'How are the kids doing?' Ruth asked.

Sheila shook her head. 'Chelsie is fuming. She's just started at college. And Alfie's gone very quiet. He's meant to be doing his GCSEs in the summer. It's such a bloody mess.'

'How do they get on with Ray?' Ruth asked.

Sheila took a few seconds to reply. 'Not good,' she admitted, pulling a face. 'They're not stupid. They know his views on stuff. Chelsie can't stand him and says he's a Nazi.'

'And Alfie?' Ruth asked.

Sheila looked a little teary again. 'They used to be so close. Alfie was like Ray's shadow. Ray managed the football team that Alfie played for. They went to watch all the Stoke home games.'

'But not anymore?' Ruth said.

Sheila shook her head. 'After one game, Alfie came home and said he didn't want to go with his dad to the games anymore.'

'Did he say why?'

'Yeah,' Sheila nodded. 'Alfie said that Ray and his mates were making comments about the black players. Even the ones that played for Stoke. And then they tried to get into a fight with some of the other team's fans.' Sheila blew out her cheeks and looked emotional. 'Alfie looked so disappointed. Ray went mad when he said he didn't want to go any more. Called him a faggot. But Alfie just refused.'

'That's sad,' Ruth said, feeling a little caught up in what Sheila was telling her.

Then Sheila looked at Ruth. 'The other officers said that I can't speak to my parents for a while. And even when I do, I'll have to make special arrangements every time we want to see them?'

'I'm afraid that's true.' Ruth nodded. 'You do understand that Ray was a member of an illegal far-right terrorist group? And the people that run that group are incredibly dangerous.'

'Terrorist?' Sheila looked shocked. 'Ray isn't a terrorist. I don't understand.'

'British Action are a terrorist organisation,' Ruth explained wondering how or if Sheila didn't know any of this.

Sheila shook her head slowly. 'I just didn't know. I swear to you.'

A figure appeared in the doorway.

It was Chelsie. She had a scowl on her face.

'I need my phone,' she snapped angrily. 'This is ridiculous. What am I supposed to do? How am I going to talk to my friends?'

Ruth looked at her. 'You're not going to be able to talk to your friends at the moment.'

'What?' Chelsie growled.

'But you will be allowed a new phone eventually,' Ruth said.

'This is bullshit!'

'We've talked about this, love,' Sheila said trying to comfort her.

'Right,' Chelsie shouted with a frustrated wave of her arms. 'I'm not staying here. You can't make me. I'm going back to Stoke.'

Ruth stood up slowly, wondering quite how she was going to handle this. 'I know this is difficult for you, Chelsie.'

'No, you don't!' she yelled. 'You don't know anything about me.'

'You can't leave, love,' Sheila sighed.

'Your mum's right,' Ruth said gently, trying to defuse the situation. 'We can't let you leave for your own safety.'

'My safety?' she snorted. 'This is nothing to do with me! This is my dad's shit. He's the one that's in danger.'

'I'm afraid that's not true,' Ruth said looking directly at you. 'The men that want to harm your dad will do anything to get to him. And that includes using you to hurt him.'

The colour drained from Chelsie's face as the gravity of the situation sunk in. 'I'm still not staying,' she mumbled as she stormed off.

Sheila pulled a face as she looked at Ruth. 'Sorry…'

'It's fine,' Ruth reassured her as she sat back down. 'I've got a daughter in her twenties. I can remember what they're like. And you've all been through a lot in recent days. Chelsie is bound to be upset.'

'Well, she still shouldn't have spoken to you like that,' Sheila insisted. 'You're just trying to help us.'

Ruth nodded, sipped her tea, still concerned about Chelsie. It was something she needed to flag up with the Witness Protection team.

CHAPTER 25

Nick and Kennedy were now sitting in Mary Kendall's living room. The air was heavy with the scent of furniture polish and something faintly lavender. It was nostalgic, almost comforting. A grandfather clock ticked steadily in the corner, its pendulum swinging in patient rhythm. Lace curtains filtered the mid-afternoon light, softening the edges of the well-kept but dated furniture.

Mary, in her early seventies, moved with a certain precision. Her short hair was neatly clipped and a blend of blonde and silver, and framed a face that had seen much but aged gracefully. Her thin-rimmed glasses caught the light as she set down a tray.

'I'm afraid I've only got Jaffa Cakes,' she said, a tinge of apology in her voice as she placed the tray on the coffee table. 'I've not managed to get out to the shops this week.'

'Don't worry, I love Jaffa Cakes,' Kennedy said with a warm smile, the kind that put people at ease.

Nick didn't usually go in for coffee and biscuits on the job. Too many wasted hours, too many half-truths offered with a custard cream. But something told him this would be worth it. Mary wasn't the type to chatter for the sake of it. And after the last twenty-four hours, he wasn't about to turn down caffeine and sugar.

'How long have you lived here, Mary?' Nick asked, taking a tentative sip of his black coffee.

Mary blinked slowly, as if calculating the years. 'Just over five years. I moved here after my husband Gerald died. I needed somewhere smaller and quieter.'

Nick nodded as his eyes wandered over the mantlepiece. One framed photo stood alone. It showed Mary and a man arm-in-arm, their smiles wide and their clothes dated. Other than that, there were no photos of children or grandchildren. A subtle silence echoed through the absence.

Kennedy, always good at shifting tone without jarring it, glanced out of the window. 'And was Ian Nesbitt living across the road from you when you moved in?'

Mary snorted, a sharp, derisive sound that didn't match her polite veneer. 'God, no. I wouldn't have moved in if *that* man was living there.'

Nick raised an eyebrow. 'You don't have much time for Mr Nesbitt?'

'No, I don't,' she said firmly. 'Horrible little man. So rude. I think he smokes marijuana. The smell sometimes comes in here if he's smoking in his garden.'

'Do you know his son Darren Nesbitt?' Kennedy asked, notebook ready.

Mary rolled her eyes, leaned back in her chair. 'Oh, yes. I know Darren. Right chip off the old block too. Loud, obnoxious, struts around like the world owes him something.'

'We're looking for Darren in connection with a very serious crime,' Nick said carefully, watching her reaction.

Mary paused. Her eyes narrowed behind the lenses. 'Not that poor MP that was shot the other day?'

'I'm afraid I can't discuss the details,' Nick said, his tone even.

Mary nodded, though her curiosity burned bright. 'I think I saw him yesterday,' she offered, then hesitated. 'But my memory's shocking these days. Could've been a few days ago. Or last week. Time blurs when you don't have anywhere to be.'

'Was he on his scooter?' Kennedy asked.

'Yes. Always on that thing. Makes a terrible racket. Sounds like a wasp in a tin can.' She nudged the plate of Jaffa Cakes closer. 'Don't let these go to waste. Gerald always said they were the perfect biscuit-cake.'

Nick allowed himself a smile and took one, absent-mindedly scanning the window again. Across the narrow road stood Ian Nesbitt's unassuming semi-detached house.

A thought stirred in his mind. 'Mary, do you have a video doorbell by any chance?'

She looked pleased to be asked. 'Oh, yes. You can't be too careful these days, can you? I got it after someone stole some of my garden furniture.'

Nick gave Kennedy a glance. The camera faced directly towards Nesbitt's house. If Darren had been there yesterday, they might have proof.

'Mind if we take a look at the footage from yesterday?' he asked.

Mary looked briefly confused, then nodded. 'Of course not. The man at the shop linked it to my computer, over there, on the desk.'

'Brilliant,' Nick said, standing up.

Mary followed them over, her slippers shuffling softly on the carpet. Nick gestured to the chair.

'Mind if I sit?'

'Be my guest. I never use it for much. Just for some emails, Ebay and the odd bit of sudoku.'

Nick sat and opened the laptop. The icon for the video system sat dead centre on the desktop. One click, and the interface appeared with blue date-stamped buttons along the side.

He selected yesterday and fast-forwarded through the morning.

'That was Terry, my window cleaner,' Mary said brightly as a face briefly flashed across the screen. 'He's always in a rush but he does a good job.'

The afternoon footage rolled by and at 15:24, a black scooter pulled up opposite.

'There he is,' Nick said, slowing the video.

They watched Darren remove his helmet and glance up and down the street. He looked anxious.

Kennedy leaned in. 'Well, now we know Ian was lying about not seeing his son.'

Nick's expression hardened. 'By my calculation, Darren drove straight here after the incident we're investigating.'

They watched in silence as Darren wheeled his scooter down the side alley of the house and vanished round the back.

Kennedy voiced what they were both thinking. 'Do we think he's still there?'

'I don't know. We searched the house but not the garden or any outbuildings.' He pressed play again and moved it on.

A few hours later, just as the light was dying, a white Luton van pulled up outside Ian's house.

'Here we go,' Nick murmured.

A man jumped out, lowered the platform on the van. A minute later, Darren reappeared, pushing his scooter.

The two men exchanged a brief, almost celebratory embrace.

'Jesus,' Nick muttered under his breath.

They loaded the scooter into the van and Darren climbed into the passenger seat.

Nick's eyes narrowed as the driver shut the rear door. 'Hold on, Sarge,' Kennedy said, pointing. 'Go back a bit. There's some writing on that shutter.'

Nick rewound and paused at the moment the door began to close. There was text, just visible, arcing across the top of the van's shutter.

'I can't read that. It's too pixelated,' Nick said in frustration.

'Might need to send it to Digital Forensics,' Kennedy suggested.

But Mary had already wandered to her bureau. She returned triumphantly with a large magnifying glass.

'Here. Try this. Gerald's from his model railway days,' she said with a glint in her eye.

'Thanks.' Nick took it, shrugged at Kennedy and leaned towards the screen.

The lettering leaped into focus.

Bowie's Cars, Metals & Scrap – 01952 770165

Nick let out a low whistle. 'Forget Digital Forensics, Mary. We just needed Sherlock Holmes.'

Mary chuckled, clearly pleased.

Kennedy scribbled the company name down. 'That's a Telford number, isn't it?'

Nick nodded. 'Yeah, I think so. And if they've taken Darren in that van, we've got a lead. But we need to move on this now.'

CHAPTER 26

It was getting dark as Ruth stood outside the safe house and gazed across at Bala Lake below. By her calculations, they were on the east side of the lake as the sun was dropping below the horizon directly in front of her. She gave a little laugh to herself. She was no Crocodile Dundee, but she felt a little sense of pride in having worked out where they were by the position of the setting sun.

The lake was a dark, inky colour. Even though it was autumn, there were several tiny figures out on the lake. Paddleboarders in wetsuits.

Jesus, rather them than me, Ruth thought, shivering at the very idea of being out there.

The air was crisp and damp, the kind of early evening that made you pull your coat collar a little tighter. A thin, reedy breeze stirred the bracken on the hillside and whispered through the narrow copse of pine trees below the track. Over to her right, fields and then moorland stretched away before climbing up the brooding slopes of Moel y Garnedd.

Despite herself, Ruth felt the familiar flicker of anxiety in her stomach. Something wasn't sitting right. It wasn't anything tangible – just a tension in the air. A stillness that had arrived too suddenly.

The metallic clink of the security gates starting to open broke her train of thought. Glancing over, she saw that a black BMW X5 was waiting to come through the gates. Inside were the officers from the Witness Protection Unit. Detective Constable Bhutto and Detective Inspector Callaghan. In the back sat Patricia Hoskins, the lawyer from the North Wales Crown Prosecution Service.

Rob was inside and must have seen them arriving via the elaborate CCTV and security set-up and opened the gates for them. They were due to finalise the plans for Clarke and his family, making explicit that he would be required to testify in court against the men from British Action that had ordered the assassination of Ashwin Choudary.

Ruth gave them a half-wave as the BMW pulled up and stopped. They all got out.

As Bhutto and Callaghan went inside, Hoskins hung back to talk to Ruth.

'How have they been?' Hoskins asked. 'The Clarkes?'

'Ray is very quiet. He hasn't done much but sit and watch TV,' Ruth explained as they walked up the stone steps into the house. 'Sheila is upset. The son, Alfie, has just sat in his room reading and playing one of those handheld video game things.'

'It's a huge change,' Hoskins said.

'It's the daughter, Chelsie, that I'm really worried about,' Ruth admitted as they walked down the long, shadowy hallway.

'Why's that?' Hoskins asked quietly.

They came to what had once been a large dining room. There was an oval meeting table with half a dozen chairs spaced around it.

'Obviously she wants to see her friends,' Ruth replied. 'She threatened to run away.'

Hoskins pulled a face. 'That's not good.'

'No,' Ruth said as they entered the room.

Rob was sitting at the top of the table looking at his tablet. Next to him were Clarke and Sheila.

Bhutto and Callaghan pulled out chairs on the far side and sat down.

Ruth and Hoskins took the final two chairs closest to the door.

Callaghan shifted his chair and looked over at Clarke and Sheila. 'Okay, we've got a few things to go over with you this evening. I know that Patricia has some paperwork that she needs you to sign, Ray. And then we need to iron out some of the specifics of you guys entering the Witness Protection scheme.'

'How long are we going to be here?' Sheila blurted out anxiously.

'You'll be here until Ray has given his testimony at trial,' Callaghan explained in a flat tone.

There were a few seconds of silence.

Rob put his tablet down, looked over and said, 'I don't know if you've seen the news, but early this morning officers from Special Crime and Counter Terrorism Division arrested two members of British Action. Neil Baker and Steve Bradshaw.' Rob looked directly at Ray. 'These are the men that you have implicated in ordering and planning the murder of Ashwin Choudary.'

Clarke nodded to confirm this but he looked terrified.

Rob then narrowed his eyes. 'There is something that I haven't asked you. Did you ever hear of a person who was known as "Wolf".'

Clarke took a short breath and nodded. 'I've heard of him. But that's about it.'

'What did you hear?'

'Nothing much.' Clarke shrugged. 'Just that he ran things. People seemed a bit scared of him.'

'And you have no idea who that person is?' Ruth asked.

'No.' Clarke shook his head adamantly. It seemed like a genuine answer. 'What about Darren Nesbitt? Why haven't you arrested him?'

'Darren is still on the run,' Ruth explained. 'My officers are currently tracking him down.'

'Right,' Clarke mumbled.

Sheila bit nervously at her nails. 'How long before Ray has to go to court then?'

Hoskins sat forward. 'We're not sure. The members of British Action will be appearing before a judge this afternoon and will put in a plea for the charges of conspiracy to commit a racially motivated crime. No doubt they will plead not guilty. Due to the severity of the crime, I'm hoping that they will be remanded into custody in prison.' Hoskins then looked over at Ruth. 'Then North Wales Police and Counter Terrorism will build as strong a case as they can against these men before that trial. And Ray's testimony will be a fundamental part of our case against them...'

'You haven't answered my question,' Sheila snapped. Her nerves were getting the better of her.

Clarke looked at them. 'Yeah. Is this weeks or months? How long are we going to be here?'

Hoskins took a moment. 'Best case scenario would be nine months.'

'Nine months,' Sheila sighed, shaking her head.

'But given the complexity of this case,' Hoskins continued, 'I would think it will be a year to eighteen months.'

'Jesus,' Sheila gasped. 'What about schools for the kids?'

'That will all be taken care of,' Bhutto explained. 'Your children will be given new identities, new birth certificates. We will then register them at new schools under these new identities. We will also create new fake school histories for them both, based on their own actual schooling.'

Sheila glared at Clarke. 'I can't believe you're putting us through all this,' she snarled at him.

Clarke put his head in his hands. 'I'm so sorry,' he whispered.

Callaghan looked over. 'We'll bring in coaches who will work with Chelsie and Alfie on their new identities. And their personal histories. As we've already explained, we will have to close and wipe clean their social media profiles.'

'Oh, my God,' Sheila said quietly. 'I feel like I'm in some hideous dream and I'm gonna wake up any second.'

'I know this is very difficult for all of you,' Ruth said gently. 'But as time goes by, you will all get used to it.'

'I don't want to get used to it!' Sheila snapped again and then her eyes filled with tears. She looked at Clarke who was staring at the floor. 'What have you done to us, Ray? What have you done?'

Clarke didn't answer.

There was a tense silence. The hum of the overhead lights seemed suddenly too loud.

'And after the trial?' Sheila asked. 'Then what?'

Bhutto looked at her tablet for a second. 'We've done some research. We've identified a town in Cornwall. St Agnes. It's a lovely little town close to the north coast of Cornwall.'

Clarke shrugged and then nodded. 'I like the sound of that,' he said as he looked at Sheila with an apologetic expression. 'What do you think, love?'

Sheila ran her hands through her hair and blew out her cheeks. 'Cornwall is miles from anywhere, Ray,' she sighed.

'Cornwall!' bellowed a voice.

Chelsie had clearly been listening from outside. She now stood at the slightly open door with her hands on her hips. 'Are you bloody kidding me! What the hell is in Cornwall?' She then threw her hands up in utter disbelief. 'I'm not going. You can't make me.' Then she gestured. 'And I'm not bloody staying here either.'

Chelsie waltzed out of the room dramatically.

Sheila went to get up.

'It's okay,' Ruth reassured her. 'I'll go and talk to her. Might be better coming from me.'

Ruth caught Jane's eye who nodded and got up too. 'I'll come with you,' Jane said gently.

Ruth and Jane came out into the hallway.

Alfie was sitting at the bottom of the stairs playing his handheld game and clearly oblivious to what was going on.

'Did you see where Chelsie went?' Ruth asked him quietly.

'Up to her room,' Alfie mumbled without taking his eyes off the screen.

'Thanks,' Jane said as they both squeezed past him and made their way up the carpeted staircase and to the landing.

'She's just here on the left,' Ruth said pointing to a door.

As they arrived at Chelsie's temporary bedroom, they saw that she was angrily folding up her clothes and putting them into a suitcase that lay open on the bed.

'Hi, Chelsie,' Ruth said in a gentle tone as she and Jane came in very slowly.

'I'm not staying,' Chelsie growled as she threw a hoodie into the case.

'Okay,' Ruth said with a nod.

Jane went and sat down in a padded chair in the corner of the room while Ruth perched on the corner of the bed.

'Chelsie, I know that this is all incredibly unfair on all of you,' Jane said in a low, empathetic tone. 'I can't begin to understand how it feels to have your whole life turned upside down like this.'

'No, you can't!' Chelsie snapped as she continued to grab her things.

'The thing is,' Ruth said, 'we can't keep your family safe if you keep saying that you're going to leave. And eventually we're going to have to take you back to Stoke.'

'Good,' Chelsie snorted. 'That's what I want.'

'But if that happens,' Jane said, 'you're going to be in danger.'

'No. My dad's messed up,' Chelsie shrugged. 'And if those men beat him up, that's his fault. I don't care. He's a prick.'

'It's not just your dad,' Ruth explained. 'Every time any of you leave the house, you're going to be looking over your shoulder to see if anyone is waiting for you or following you. Every time your stepmum goes shopping. Every time the doorbell rings. Every time you hear a strange noise outside your house at night.'

Chelsie shook her head. 'But we haven't done anything,' she huffed – but what they were telling her had some effect because she'd stopped packing.

'Chelsie, you seem like a very intelligent young woman,' Jane stated. 'Your dad is going to go to court to testify against these men and say that they were involved in a murder.'

Chelsie gave her a withering a look. 'I know that.'

Ruth looked directly at her. 'And those men are going to do anything to stop him doing that. They might hurt your dad. But they might also threaten to hurt you, your stepmum or your brother. And as horrible as it sounds, they might hurt one of you just to stop your dad going to court.'

'Alfie?' Chelsie asked sceptically as if this had only just occurred to her.

Ruth nodded with a serious expression. 'Any of you.'

Chelsie bit at her nails and took a deep breath. Her hands shook slightly. For some reason, she just hadn't thought that Alfie was in danger. Ruth's words had provoked something deeper than anger.

'Why don't you stop packing for a bit and come downstairs?' Jane suggested in a kind voice.

Chelsie didn't answer right away. But she stopped folding the clothes. Her shoulders had slumped. And that, Ruth thought, was something.

Ruth stood up slowly and crossed the room to sit beside her.

'It's not fair,' she whispered.

'I know it's not,' Ruth said. 'None of this is fair.'

There was a long pause.

'I didn't even get to say goodbye to my friends,' Chelsie murmured. 'One minute I was in school... the next we're in a car with blacked-out windows and told never to look back. I didn't even tell Ellie. She'll think I just ghosted her.'

'I'm sorry,' Ruth said quietly. She wanted to offer more – but there was nothing that would make this easier.

Chelsie looked down at the jumper still clutched in her hands. Her lip trembled. 'I hate him sometimes... my dad. I really do. But I still don't want him to die. And I don't want Alfie to get hurt. I don't want to be scared forever.'

Ruth nodded. 'Then stay. Let us help you.'

Chelsie finally met her eyes. For a moment, she looked like a child again.

'Why don't you come downstairs for a bit?' Jane suggested in a virtual whisper.

Chelsie gave the faintest of nods and got up.

They all moved slowly towards the door.

The suitcase lay open and forgotten on the bed.

Outside, the last of the daylight slipped behind the hills, and a hush settled over the house.

And Ruth, quietly, took that as a win.

CHAPTER 27

The night pressed in cold and brittle around the safe house. Ruth stood outside and wrapped a scarf around her to keep warm. The grey slate tiles of the roof glinted slightly in the hard light of the moon.

Ruth moved down the edge of the gravel driveway, turning her collar up against the sharp chill that rolled in off Bala Lake. The water stretched out like glass – black and glistening. The outline of the Snowdonia mountains in the distance cut sharp against the clear, star-pricked sky.

A cigarette glowed between Ruth's fingers. She dragged on it, the ember glowing angrily in the darkness. Smoke curled upwards and caught the moonlight before dissolving.

Behind her, the safe house loomed.

The crunch of footsteps on the gravel made her turn.

Clarke emerged from the shadows, shoulders hunched, hands buried deep in the pockets of a puffer jacket.

'Can't sleep?' she asked him.

The security light clicked on with his movement.

'No,' he mumbled. His eyes flitted to hers, wary. He sat down on the nearby stone wall. The sag of regret, the weight of what he'd done heavy on him. Then he stared out at the lake as if might swallow him, save him, if he looked long enough.

'It was never meant to be like this,' Clarke said. His words were low and strained. 'What happened to Choudary. It's not why I got involved with them.'

'So, what happened?' Ruth asked as she finished her cigarette.

Clarke shook his head as he struggled to find the words to explain. 'It was about standing up for ourselves. Protecting your own. We've got nothing and they get given everything.'

Ruth frowned. 'They?'

'Immigrants,' Clarke said as if it was obvious.

There's that word again, Ruth thought. But she wasn't going to be drawn into a conversation about her own views on immigration. It wasn't appropriate or necessary.

'White working class. We're the bloody minority,' Clarke said as if talking to himself.

Ruth studied him in profile. The stubble, the pale skin, crow's feet etched around the eyes. Clarke was tired, confused and scared.

Ruth let the silence stretch between them. The sound of the water lapping at the shore drifted up, faint but insistent. Her cigarette hissed as she stubbed it out against the low stone wall.

'All I know is that there is a wife and her children who have lost their father,' Ruth said very quietly. 'And they're in a great deal of pain and anguish.'

Clarke didn't respond. He just stared out at the lake, his shoulders sagging further under the weight of it all. The cold, inescapable facts of what he'd done. What he'd been responsible for.

CHAPTER 28

It was early morning and Nick and Kennedy had driven over to Bowie's Cars, Metal and Scrap yard that was somewhere between Shifnal and Telford in Shropshire. It was in the middle of nowhere. Having spotted a hill that overlooked the yard, Nick and Kennedy had climbed to the top to observe what was going on before they went in.

A still mist clung low over the hilltop.

Grabbing his binoculars, Nick used the plastic central focusing wheel to bring everything into sharp view. Beyond the skeletal fence, heaps of twisted metal rose in silent, corroded mounds – rusted car doors, crumpled sheets of corrugated iron.

'Anything?' Kennedy asked, though her voice was barely more than a murmur.

Nick took the binoculars from his face for a moment. 'Nothing yet,' he admitted in a frustrated tone as he pulled his coat tighter, the damp seeping into the dark, navy wool, and into his bones.

Scouring the yard, Nick's eyes narrowed on the endless shadowy lines of tangled metal that were eerie and still. Then he moved the binoculars, fixing on the entrance gates that had been open since they'd arrived. It seemed unusual unless someone was inside the yard already.

A gull screeched somewhere overhead, the sound raw and sudden in the muffled stillness.

Then Nick spotted movement.

A figure walking from behind of a line of rusty farm machinery towards the long line of blue, single-storey Portakabins.

Darren Nesbitt!

'Bingo!' Nick hissed as he moved the binoculars and looked at Kennedy. 'Nesbitt,' he said handing them to her.

'At least we know he's there,' Kennedy said as she looked, before handing them back to Nick.

As Nick looked again, he saw two figures appearing from the Portakabins. One tall and wiry. The other was stockier with a greasy ponytail.

'Okay, we've got two more men down there,' Nick said to Kennedy. Then he spotted what they were carrying by their sides.

Sawn-off shotguns.

'Shit,' Nick hissed. 'And they've got firearms. Sawn-offs.'

The thin wiry man now cradled the shotgun with the easy familiarity of someone who'd used it before.

As they all turned back towards the Portakabins, the mist lifted as the wind picked up.

Nick put down the binoculars and gave Kennedy a dark look. 'We going to need to come back with arrest and search warrants. And Armed Response Units.'

Kennedy didn't say anything at first. Just met Nick's look and gave a single nod. No bravado. Just the tight, cold understanding of what this meant.

Below them, the men had vanished inside the Portakabins.

Kennedy crouched beside him, eyes scanning the yard one last time. 'They'll be armed and cornered. And they won't run. Not types like that. Fanatics.'

'No,' Nick agreed in a dark tone.

CHAPTER 29

Ruth came into the kitchen with her phone in her hand. The smell of coffee lingered beneath the sharper tang of disinfectant. Jane and Rob were over by the kettle, their shoulders hunched slightly, voices low as they busied themselves.

'Two of my officers have spotted Darren Nesbitt in a scrap metal yard near Telford,' Ruth explained, holding up her phone like evidence. 'I've actioned search and arrest warrants. We've got a Tactical Firearms Unit going in, so I'm hoping Nesbitt will be in custody before midday.'

Jane gave a grim smile, lifting her hand with crossed fingers. 'I don't suppose he'll tell us anything but getting him off the streets will be a relief.'

Rob poured boiling water into the mugs, steam curling up around him. 'A desperate man with a firearm is never good,' he muttered.

'Actually, there's several armed men there,' Ruth admitted. 'I'm sending in a full ARU with my officers.'

'Right. Sounds heavy.' Rob looked over with a serious expression. 'Keep us posted.'

'I will do.'

'Can I make you a coffee?' he asked.

For a moment Ruth hesitated, the comforting image of her usual morning flat white flickering in her mind. Normality felt distant this morning, almost unreachable. 'Okay. Yes. Please. Milk, no sugar.'

A faint shuffle behind her made Ruth turn. Sheila hovered in the doorway, wrapped in a pink dressing gown that had seen better days. Her hair was unbrushed, her face pale, eyes tight with worry.

'Everything all right?' Ruth asked, though the answer was already in Sheila's expression.

'Anyone seen Chelsie this morning?' Sheila's voice was small but laced with fear.

Ruth's stomach dropped. She looked to Rob and Jane, but they both shook their heads, faces hardening with concern.

'She's not in her bedroom?' Jane asked, already sounding as if she knew the answer.

'No,' Sheila whispered. 'And I've checked the bathroom.'

Ruth's pulse quickened, instincts kicking in like a switch flicked. Without another word, she strode out of the kitchen, every step sharp with purpose.

The hallway was cold, the silence heavy. Ruth pushed open the meeting room door. Empty. The chairs still neatly pushed in, the table untouched.

She checked the living room next, hoping that she'd find Chelsie sprawled on the sofa, lost in some dreadful morning TV. But the room was silent.

Her chest tightened. *This isn't good.*

Back in the hallway, Rob and Jane were already there with grim expressions.

'I've tried the downstairs toilet,' Rob reported quietly.

'She's not in the utility room,' Jane added.

Ruth's eyes flicked between them, a tremor in her voice. 'Then where the bloody hell is she?'

CHAPTER 30

Nick sat in the back of the Armed Response Vehicle, the hum of the engine barely cutting through the cold, sterile air inside. For the last ten minutes, the vehicle had been hidden behind a feed shed on a desolate, disused farm, a perfect location for them to lie low before the operation. Now, as the armoured BMW X5 crept out and turned towards Bowie's scrapyard, a sense of unease settled over him.

Inside the ARV, the air was thick with tension. Nick shared the cramped space with four Armed Response Officers, their movements slow and deliberate as they adjusted their gear, their eyes fixed ahead. Clad in black helmets, dark goggles and the unforgiving weight of Kevlar vests, they were ready for whatever came next. The weight of their weapons – the G36C assault rifles, the dark shadows they cast under the light – was a visible reminder of the firepower at their disposal. Each officer's hands were on the weapons, fingers grazing the triggers almost unconsciously. The rifles, with their 100-round C-Mag drum magazines, could rip through a target at an unimaginable rate of 750 rounds per minute.

Nick gripped the leather strap hanging from the roof, steadying himself as the vehicle turned, a jolt of motion shooting through him. The adrenaline, sharp and electric, surged through his veins, heightening every sense. He could feel the nervous energy radiating from the officers beside him, their muscles tight, prepared. The hum of the Tetra radio, the intermittent crackle of static, broke the otherwise suffocating silence. The voice of Gold Command, low and gravelly, offered instructions, the words almost muffled in the air of tension.

The smell inside the vehicle was sharp – gun oil, sweat and the stale tang of cigarettes. It wasn't a place for conversation. But when the young ARO sitting next to him shifted, chewing gum with mechanical precision, the faintest hint of mint filled the car for a moment. He glanced at Nick, his face hidden behind a balaclava, his eyes alert, locking with Nick's gaze. 'You okay, sir?' The voice was thick with a Yorkshire accent.

Nick smirked, the sarcasm coming naturally. 'Never better.'

The young officer gave him a brief, almost nervous grin. 'Just keep behind us, eh? We don't want you having to use that thing.' He gestured to Nick's Glock 19, holstered at his side.

Nick returned the grin, but there was no humour in it. The idea of firing his weapon didn't sit right with him. The weight of it, the responsibility. No one liked using their firearm unless they absolutely had to.

The vehicle slowed as they neared their destination. The driver spoke into the radio, his voice calm but firm. 'Gold Command, Gold Command. Sierra Oscar Five, are you receiving, over?'

The radio crackled to life, Gold Command's voice cutting through the static. 'Gold Command to Sierra Oscar Five. Receiving, go ahead. Over.'

The driver's response was crisp and businesslike. 'Sierra Oscar Five. We have arrived at the target destination. Out.' A pause. 'Standby.'

The BMW came to a stop. Nick got out, his pulse racing.

The yard sprawled out in every direction, filled with towering heaps of rusted car parts, battered scrap metal and broken machinery.

There was an eerie stillness in the air, punctuated only by the distant hum of wind whipping through the derelict structures.

Nick's breath felt shallow. *This doesn't feel right.*

He moved with purpose, but there was a certain unease gnawing at the back of his thoughts.

In their well-practised stance, the AROs fanned out, their bodies low and quiet as they closed in on the warehouse's flank wall.

Suddenly, two large black ravens burst from the shadows behind the door, the sound of their wings cutting through the air.

It's too quiet, Nick thought, clenching his jaw. *This is wrong. Where are they all? Are they just lying in wait to ambush us?*

Nick glanced over at Kennedy. She gave him a shrug as if to say *Where is everyone?*

The AROs continued to move methodically, their movements deliberate as they spread out, ensuring there was no escape route.

'It's deserted,' Nick said, his voice low, barely audible.

Kennedy didn't answer immediately, instead casting a look at the silent warehouse, her eyes narrowing with suspicion.

Nick moved towards the large warehouse door.

AROs went inside.

'Armed police!' they bellowed. 'Show yourselves.'

Nothing.

Nick glanced over to his right.

Two AROs were checking the Portakabins, kicking open the doors and shouting their warnings, machine guns held tight into their shoulders.

After a few more seconds, the lead ARO came out of the warehouse. He looked over at the two AROs who were standing by the Portakabins.

They gave him a signal to show that they were clear.

The lead ARO then glanced at Nick. 'Sorry, sir. There's no one here.'

Kennedy gave Nick a dark look.

'They knew we were coming,' she growled angrily.

'Yeah, they did,' Nick agreed. 'But how?'

CHAPTER 31

The search for Chelsie had now progressed to the sizeable garden and small wooded area at the back of the safe house. Above that, the ground continued to climb upwards to the top of a ridge.

'Chelsie?' Sheila called loudly.

Looking into the dark woods, Ruth strained her eyesight as she looked for the slightest sign of movement. The sunlight fell in little shards and slices through the gaps in the canopy of trees, casting long shadows across the forest floor.

Rob jogged over. 'Nothing around the front. The security gates are closed and locked.'

Jane joined them, a little out of breath. 'Nothing on the other side either.'

Ruth glanced around. The thick walls around the garden had anti-climb spikes on top of them for added security. 'Well, she didn't climb over those, did she?' Ruth said, thinking to herself. The air around them seemed unnervingly still. There was the hum of a distant tractor somewhere in the distance.

Rob gestured to the woods. 'Then she's got to be in there somewhere.'

Sheila came over, her face stricken with concern. 'I don't understand where she can be.'

Jane nodded towards the trees. 'We think she might be in there. It's the only place we haven't searched properly.'

The dense undergrowth made the woods feel ominous, the air cool and damp beneath the towering trees. The place seemed endless, the shadows playing tricks on their eyes.

'Bloody girl,' Sheila huffed, wiping her brow with the back of her hand. 'She'll be the death of me.' The frustration in her voice was evident, but so was the worry. They had been searching for half an hour now.

They all turned and started along a narrow pathway that was littered with autumnal leaves, the crunching sound beneath their feet loud in the silence.

'Chelsie!' Rob bellowed in a deep, loud voice, his frustration mounting. His words echoed through the woods.

Ruth felt her stomach knot. Her mind raced. They had checked every other possible place. This was it – the woods were the last hope, the last place they hadn't fully combed through. What if she wasn't here? What if she had managed to get away and was now trying to get back to her home in Stoke? The thought made her blood run cold.

Out of the corner of her eye, Ruth spotted something.

A figure moving from behind some trees about twenty yards away.

'She's over there,' Jane shouted.

'Oh, thank God,' Sheila gasped.

'Chelsie!' Ruth shouted over at her.

Chelsie gave them a nonchalant wave as she made her way casually through the trees and down the path towards them.

'Where have you been?' Sheila demanded angrily.

Chelsie pulled a face of disdain. 'Erm, I went for a walk. There's nothing else to do,' she said defiantly.

'We've been looking everywhere for you,' Sheila continued.

Chelsie shrugged. 'Well, I'm here.'

Rob looked at her. 'If you're going for a walk out here, it would be good if you could tell someone next time. That's all,' he explained calmly, with no hint of judgement.

'You were all asleep,' Chelsie snorted witheringly. 'But okay.'

Ruth gave Jane an amused look.

By the time they reached the garden again, Clarke was standing looking very concerned.

'It's all right, Ray. Chelsie decided to go for a walk. She just didn't think to tell anyone, did you?' Sheila explained with more than a hint of sarcasm.

Ray shook his head. Her words hadn't alleviated his anxiety. 'It's not Chelsie I'm worried about. It's Alfie. I've searched everywhere. He's vanished.'

CHAPTER 32

It was an hour later by the time Ruth, Rob and Jane entered the small security control room on the ground floor of the safe house. It had a desk with three computer monitors that were linked to the dozen or so security cameras positioned both inside and outside the house. There were a bank of multi-coloured switches that operated the security lights plus a sophisticated alarm system that was linked to all the doors and the half-dozen or so panic buttons scattered through the property. A small sign was fixed to the wall that read *Security Code – Front gates – #2794#*.

'Jesus,' Jane muttered under her breath, scanning the room like it might bite her. 'This doesn't look like any safe house I've ever been to before.'

'That's MI5 for you,' Rob explained as he sat down at the desk, fingers already moving to wake the dormant screens.

Jane frowned. 'Do we think that Alfie just somehow got over the walls and has done a runner back home?'

Ruth shrugged, dragging over an office chair and plonking herself down. 'We've searched everywhere. There's part of me hoping that he's done a runner rather than... anything more sinister.'

Rob tapped away at the computer, the clicks loud in the tensioned air. He tried to access the video files from last night. Whatever had happened to Alfie, and however he'd left the location of the safe house, it would be there on the security cameras for them to see.

For a moment, Ruth was taken back to a case she'd worked a few years ago. Llancastell CID had been tasked with protecting an Islamic terrorist called Abu Habib. She and Nick had been holed up with him in an MI5 safe house in the middle of Snowdonia. The memory flashed in shards: the claustrophobia, the standoff, the gunfire hammering like hail against the walls. It was probably the scariest twenty-four hours of Ruth's life.

'Here we go,' Rob said, pointing to the screen.

Jane perched on the arm of a two-seated sofa, jaw tight. Ruth wheeled her chair closer.

The screen was filled with CCTV footage from a security camera mounted on the front of the house, overlooking the driveway and gates. The timecode flickered: twelve thirty-five a.m. Rob played the footage forward, fast.

At one fifty-seven a.m., headlights.

Rob slowed the footage. A dark van at the gates. The tension in the room tripled.

The passenger door opened.

A figure dressed all in black – hoodie, balaclava, gloves – darted out. He moved with purpose.

'Are you bloody kidding me?' Rob growled.

The figure punched in the security code and the gates slid open.

'How the hell...' Jane said, her voice trailing into nothing, eyes locked on the screen.

Three masked figures jumped out. The one at the keypad looked straight into the camera. Not a glance – *a stare*.

Then he pulled out a can of spray paint.

Ruth's stomach clenched.

A Nazi salute.

He sprayed the paint in violent arcs and the video feed went black.

'Bloody hell,' Jane growled.

'It's okay,' Rob said quickly, already switching feeds. 'There's a camera mounted on the roof.'

Ruth's thoughts spiralled. It didn't matter. She already knew what they'd see next.

'Here we go,' Rob said again, a grim undertone in his voice.

From the higher angle, the van's side panel was clearer. Rob froze the frame as Ruth grabbed her phone.

'Boss?' Garrow answered.

The three figures moved quickly on-screen. Ruth's voice tightened. 'Jim, we have a major problem.'

'Okay,' Garrow said.

'I need you to run a plate,' she said. Her voice was level, but her pulse pounded. 'Alpha-lima-one-five, tango-yankee-oscar. It's a navy Ford Transit van.'

'What's going on, boss?'

Ruth didn't answer straight away. On-screen, the figures emerged again, dragging someone hooded towards the van.

Her heart dropped. Those trackies and trainers. She knew them.

Alfie.

Oh, God.

'Ray Clarke's son Alfie has just been taken. One fifty-seven a.m. By members of British Action, I think.'

'From the safe house?' Garrow said, stunned.

'Yes,' Ruth sighed. 'I've got a missed call from Nick. What happened over in Telford?'

'Waste of time,' Garrow replied. 'Place was dead. Nick thinks they were tipped off.'

Ruth's jaw tensed. Her mind kicked into overdrive.

'Tell him to call me. And run that plate – but it's probably stolen.'

'On it, boss.'

Ruth ended the call and sat back, staring at the now-empty screen.

There was a leak.

The words thudded in her head like a drumbeat.

A leak.

She scanned Jane. Then Rob.

Who the hell had given the kidnappers their location and the code?

CHAPTER 33

'Right, listen up, everyone,' Nick said, raising his voice a notch as he strode across the CID office towards the scene boards. 'This is a fast-moving investigation,' he continued, gesturing at the array of photos and scribbled notes pinned under harsh fluorescent light. 'I need everyone up to speed.' He tapped a blurry CCTV still with the end of a capped marker. A navy-blue Ford Transit van dominated the centre. 'Ray Clarke's son, Alfie. He's fifteen years old and was kidnapped by three masked members of British Action at approximately two oh-four a.m. We've confirmed the van used in the abduction. The plate's stolen. I'd bet money they've switched vehicles already, maybe more than once. But this is the image we've got.' He moved to a second board, this one featuring grainy headshots and some crisp prints from Counter Terrorism. 'These are our suspects. Counter Terrorism have passed on their full intel package. The three men responsible are in these photos. Somewhere out there, likely holed up, possibly armed. Let's not forget what British Action stands for or what they're capable of.' He scanned the team, his gaze sharp. 'We're splitting into two teams. One tracks Darren Nesbitt. The other finds Alfie. I'm going to be liaising with Rob from the CTD who is at the safe house in Bala. I have also requested additional officers, but until we get them, it's just us. I know you'll give this everything you've got. But I also need you all to be vigilant. Someone told British Action the location and the code to the security gates. And Jade and I are convinced that someone also tipped off Darren Nesbitt and his goons that we were raiding Bowie's scrapyard this morning. So, everything we're working on stays within these four walls. Is that understood?'

There were murmurs of agreement from the assembled team.

Kennedy leaned forward, ponytail swinging. 'All police units across North Wales and surrounding counties are on alert. They've got the suspect photos, vehicle info, the whole works. Checks are happening as we speak.'

Nick gave a tight nod. 'Good. British Action will have taken Alfie somewhere safe. Somewhere they control. We need to dig deep. Look for intel on possible meeting locations, old haunts, lockups. Anywhere they might think is off our radar.'

Garrow raised his hand, voice steady. 'Much of their known activity is clustered around Stoke. That's our most promising lead geographically.'

'I've already spoken with Staffordshire Police,' Nick replied. 'They're aware and on standby.'

'I ran an ANPR sweep on the stolen plate,' Kennedy added, eyes flicking to her screen. 'I'm still waiting on Traffic for a hit…' She paused mid-sentence. 'Hang on. They've just sent something through.'

She clicked the mouse. The wall-mounted monitor sparked to life. Static, then footage.

ANPR CAMERA: OCTAGON RETAIL PARK – 06:21 AM

Nick stepped closer as the image sharpened. The blue Transit van pulled into a near-empty car park and slowed to a crawl. It nosed into a bay at the far end, close to a grey Luton van already parked up.

'Octagon Retail Park. That's Stoke,' Garrow confirmed, peering at his own monitor.

'Looks like a handover,' Nick murmured.

On the screen, two figures climbed out of the Transit, scanned their surroundings, then unlocked the back of the Luton.

Kennedy frowned, eyes narrowing. 'Sarge?'

Nick had already seen it.

'That's Bowie's scrapyard branding on the Luton,' he said grimly. 'Same van that picked up Darren Nesbitt from his father's place.'

The camera footage showed a third figure, who was hooded and tied up, being yanked from the Transit and pushed roughly into the Luton. The back slammed shut.

Alfie Clarke.

Kennedy muttered, 'Jesus. He's just a kid.'

Nick scratched at his beard, the bristles rasping under his fingers. 'Maybe they're heading back to Bowie's scrapyard?'

'And maybe they think we won't come back,' Kennedy said aloud.

The room fell into a focused silence. Somewhere behind them, a printer whirred to life.

'Jade, can you get onto Traffic. I want every ANPR hit on that Luton in the last twenty-four hours,' Nick said.

He turned back to the screen. The final frame showed the van disappearing from view.

'And let's find Alfie before they disappear for good.'

CHAPTER 34

Ruth entered the meeting room in the safe house carrying a tray of coffees and teas. Clarke and Sheila were sitting together at one end, utterly shellshocked by the news that their son Alfie had been kidnapped. Jane was sitting on the far side, tapping at her tablet. Rob had gone elsewhere to make urgent phone calls and liaise with Nick and Llancastell CID to co-ordinate the two operations. Ruth trusted Nick implicitly. He was more than capable of stepping into her shoes over at Llancastell. It wouldn't be long, she suspected, before Nick was promoted to Detective Inspector himself.

But even Nick couldn't help with what was gnawing away at her gut now – because Ruth was acutely aware that there was a leak somewhere in the investigation. And it wasn't just instinct; she had hard evidence. Someone was feeding these scumbags intel. Someone on the inside.

She didn't like that thought. It made her stomach twist.

'Here we go,' Ruth said gently as she put the tray down on the table.

Sheila looked up at her with a desperate expression, her eyes swollen and red from crying.

'It's okay,' Ruth said in a steady voice, forcing calm into her tone. 'We're going to find Alfie and get him back safely. I promise you.'

Sheila shook her head. 'You don't know that,' she said, her voice cracking as tears welled up again. 'Those men are animals. I can't bear to think how scared he must be. I feel sick.'

Clarke went to put a reassuring hand on his wife's shoulder, but she flinched away and glared at him.

'Don't touch me,' she snarled. 'This is all your fault.'

Jane glanced over. 'I've got a message from the NPAS,' she said. 'They're sending over two choppers to help the search. They'll be in the area within an hour.'

The National Police Air Service – the NPAS – was the unit that supplied air support to police forces across England and Wales.

Ruth nodded. 'It's good news. The helicopters will allow us to focus the search. I've spoken to my team in Llancastell. Alfie and the men switched vans just north of Stoke this morning. We've got the description and the licence plate of the new vehicle. North Wales Police and Staffordshire units are combing the area.'

A tense silence settled across the room. Ruth's eyes flicked to Clarke. His breathing was shallow and his eyes roamed the space.

'It was a mistake,' he mumbled, barely audible.

Ruth and Jane shared a glance. Something about his tone unsettled her.

'This was a big mistake,' he said again, louder this time, voice trembling. 'I can't do this.'

Jane leaned in. 'We're going to get Alfie back, Ray,' she said gently. 'It's just a matter of time.'

'No.' Clarke shook his head and looked at Sheila. 'I'm so sorry,' he whispered. 'I should have just kept quiet, shouldn't I?'

Sheila nodded slowly. 'Yes,' she murmured. 'I don't know how I let you talk us into this.'

Ruth raised a hand, attempting to defuse the escalating emotion. 'Okay, but let's not do anything hasty. I think...'

'I know these men,' Clarke interrupted. 'If I don't agree to drop my testimony... if I don't retract everything I've told you, they're going to hurt Alfie. Or worse.'

A horrible silence followed.

Sheila reached over and took his hand, her voice low and deadened. 'You have to stop all this, Ray. We have to get Alfie back, go home and you just need to keep your mouth shut.'

Jane shot Ruth an uneasy look.

'Ray, I understand how frightening this must be,' Ruth said, keeping her tone soft but firm. 'But I'm going to be honest with you. I don't think withdrawing your testimony is going to make your family any safer. I think you've gone too far down the road for these men to ever trust you again.'

The colour drained from Clarke's face. The weight of her words hit him hard.

'No,' Sheila said quickly, her voice almost pleading. 'That's not true. If you keep your mouth shut, we'll get Alfie back safely and we can go home.'

Clarke's eyes darted back and forth. 'I don't know,' he muttered. 'Maybe she's right. Maybe it's too late.'

'This is bullshit!' an angry voice cut in.

Ruth turned. It was Chelsie, Alfie's older sister, hovering in the doorway like a storm cloud. It wasn't the first time she'd been lurking nearby, listening in.

'The only thing that matters is that you find my brother,' Chelsie snapped, her face contorted in fury. 'What are you even doing sitting here? Why aren't you out there looking for him? That's your job, isn't it?'

Before Ruth could respond, her phone rang. She glanced down. It was Nick.

Ruth stood up and held the phone to her ear, manoeuvring past Chelsie.

'Boss,' Nick said, urgency clear in his voice.

'What is it?' she asked.

'Uniformed patrol have spotted the Luton van we believe Alfie is being held in,' he explained. 'It's parked outside a Travelodge just outside Stoke. It's been there for the past hour. Two men were seen walking to the petrol station nearby, bought food and drinks. They're back in the van.'

Ruth felt her pulse quicken. 'Maybe they're planning to hold him in a hotel room,' she said aloud, half-thinking.

'That was my initial thought,' Nick replied. 'Me and Jade are en route now. I'll keep you posted.'

'Right. Thank you,' Ruth said, ending the call.

She turned back to the room, all eyes fixed on her. The air was brittle with tension.

'The van we believe Alfie is in has been spotted at a hotel car park outside Stoke. My team are closing in,' Ruth explained.

There was a beat of silence.

Ruth could feel her stomach clench a little. She knew that they were running out of time. And someone inside the investigation was working against them. But if they could rescue Alfie then maybe she could get everything back on track.

CHAPTER 35

Nick looked through his binoculars across the huge service station car park, focusing in on the Luton van that was still parked outside the Travelodge Hotel. He saw a plume of vape smoke escape through a half-open window on the driver's side.

Taking the binoculars down, he looked at Kennedy and the four uniformed police officers from the Staffordshire Force.

'Looks like they're still in there,' Nick observed.

The nearest uniformed officer – twenties, blond beard, milky skin – nodded. 'They haven't moved since they came back from the petrol station, sir.'

A black Mercedes SUV with tinted windows drew up beside them.

Nick looked over. It was the Tactical Firearms Unit that he'd spoken to while he was en route to Stoke.

The lead Armed Response Officer – forties, stocky, thick-necked – jumped out of the passenger side and walked towards them.

'DS Evans?' the ARO asked.

'Yes,' Nick nodded and then handed the ARO his binoculars and pointed. 'Target vehicle is that Luton van. Two suspects in the front. We believe our kidnap Alfie is in the back, possibly with another suspect.'

The ARO nodded as he looked and then handed the binoculars back to Nick. 'And you think these men are armed?'

'I think we need to go on that assumption,' Nick replied. 'Myself and DC Kennedy will drive over and park just to the right of the van. If you guys then get into position while we do that, then I'll give the word when we can move in.'

'Right you are,' the ARO said calmly. He then looked at the uniformed officer. 'I'm going to need you to seal off that entrance,' he explained, pointing across the car park. 'We can't have any traffic coming in. And stop any pedestrians who are trying to return to their vehicles in that section of the car park. But don't make a song and dance about it.'

Nick saw the uniformed officer bristle at the slightly patronising tone of the ARO. But that was 'Shots' – police slang for armed officers – for you. They thought they were the cavalry and were mockingly referred to as 'Call of Duty Commandos' by other officers.

'I think we can handle all that,' he said with a forced smile.

A gust of wind picked up, rattling a plastic sign nearby.

'Right, let's get on with it, before they decide to leave,' Nick said with a sense of urgency, and gestured towards his car. 'Shall we?'

Nick and Kennedy got into the car and pulled away.

'Okay?' Nick asked Kennedy as they drove slowly through the car park so they could loop around to the next section where the Luton was parked.

She gave a shrug. 'I'm just thinking about Alfie in the back of that van. And all those armed officers. It just made me shudder for a moment.'

Nick nodded in agreement. 'Yeah. We just need him out of there as quickly as possible.'

Turning the steering wheel right, Nick could feel that his palms were sweaty and his pulse was quickening. He knew how quickly an operation could go wrong with deadly consequence. It could happen in the blink of an eye.

A few seconds later, Nick drove slowly past the Luton van and then pulled into an empty space parallel to them about two spaces down. He clocked that the two men were still inside. The man in the passenger seat was reading a newspaper.

He turned off the ignition.

Kennedy buzzed down her window as she and Nick pretended to have an innocuous conversation and not glance across at the Luton.

For a few seconds, they just listened.

There was no noise coming from the back of the van. But then again, if Alfie was bound and gagged, he wouldn't be able to move or shout for help anyway.

Nick stared at the reflection of the van in the rear-view mirror. His breathing had slowed, but not from calm. It was the heavy silence before a storm.

Taking a deep breath, Nick glanced at Kennedy. His heart was now pounding against his chest like a drum. 'Ready?' he asked her.

She nodded as she unclipped her seatbelt. She looked anxious.

With a surreptitious glance to his left, Nick made sure that the driver of the Luton was looking their way.

Nick grabbed the Tetra radio. 'Gold Command to all units, move in on target vehicle. I repeat, move in on target vehicle.'

Then he glanced in the rear-view mirror and took a deep breath.

This was going to need precision timing. Alfie's safety was paramount.

The Armed Response Vehicle sped into view, braking hard behind the Luton van.

'Here we go,' Nick said as he and Kennedy jumped out of the car and wheeled around towards the Luton.

In a well-rehearsed manoeuvre, the AROs in their black clothing, Kevlar vests, helmets and balaclavas moved swiftly.

Two AROs jogged around to the driver's side, their powerful Heckler & Koch G36C sub-machine guns locked into their shoulders. Two AROs fanned to the passenger side.

'Armed police! Show me your hands and get out of the vehicle slowly!' one of the AROs bellowed loudly.

'Get out! Now!' another thundered.

Nick and Kennedy joined the final two AROs at the roller shutter door at the back of the Luton van. It was locked with a thick padlock.

There was a banging sound of movement from inside the van.

Is that Alfie?

Nick's breathing was shallow.

He watched an ARO move in with a huge set of bolt cutters and snap the padlock in one swift movement.

Catching the ARO's glance, Nick moved closer to the roller shutter door.

The AROs stood, legs slightly apart, guns trained on whatever or whoever was inside the back of the van.

Nick gave them a nod as he threw the roller shutter door to reveal the back of the van.

'Armed police! Show yourselves now!' the ARO screamed.

The back of the van was cluttered with a couple of old washing machines, a stack of steel pipes, ladders, etc.

A moment of silence.

There was someone in there but they were clearly hiding.

'Armed police! Show yourselves now!' the ARO thundered as they moved closer to the back of the van.

Nick frantically scanned the contents looking for any sign of Alfie. Nothing.

Suddenly, a man – fifties, cropped hair, tattoos – moved from behind a fridge-freezer unit.

He was holding a sawn-off shotgun at his hip which was aimed at them.

Oh, shit!

Nick instinctively moved back, using the side of the van as cover.

He looked at Kennedy who had done the same.

The AROs reacted, bracing themselves.

'Drop the weapon!'

The cropped-haired man had a wild look in his eyes.

Where the hell is Alfie? Is he tied up at the back behind all the junk?

'DROP THE WEAPON OR I'LL SHOOT!'

The cropped-hair man gave a sarcastic smile and shook his head.

'Fuck off, pigs!' he snarked.

BANG!

The shotgun exploded. An orange FLASH from both barrels.

Jesus!

Nick hit the floor.

CRACK! CRACK! CRACK!

Nick looked up from the ground, slightly winded.

The AROs were still standing. 'Shots fired. Suspect down!'

An eerie silence.

'Urgent medical assistance required,' the ARO shouted as they jumped into the back of the van.

Nick scrambled to his feet, the palms of his hands grazed and bloody. But there was only one thing on his mind.

Where's Alfie?

Leaping into the back of the van, Nick saw the man lying on his back.

There were three dark red holes in the middle of his torso. Clinical precision.

Urgent medical assistance wasn't going to save him.

He was dead.

Nick sprinted to the back of the van, pulling a washing machine out of the way with a grunt.

Nothing.

Glancing over at the AROs, he saw them searching. Then they looked over and shook their heads.

Kennedy joined him. 'Anything?'

Nick took a breath as he scanned the van. Then he shook his head in frustration. 'No. He's not here.'

Kennedy gave him a dark look. 'Then where the hell is he?'

CHAPTER 36

Ruth took a cigarette from the packet, popped it in her mouth and lit it, shielding the flame from the bitter wind that blew in from Bala Lake. It was her third cigarette of the day. More than usual. Maybe it was the stress of the morning. Or being away from her usual habitat – the CID offices at Llancastell nick – that was unsettling her.

Ruth took a few steps forward so that she stood at the edge of the tree line, her boots sinking into the damp carpet of fallen leaves. The scent of woodsmoke drifted from a distant farmhouse, mingling with the earthy musk of wet bracken and decaying foliage.

Beyond the trees, Bala Lake stretched cold and silver under a pewter sky. Its surface barely rippled, save for a lone cormorant skimming low over the water, wings cutting through the silence. The mountains of Snowdonia loomed in the distance, jagged silhouettes draped in the season's mist, their upper reaches brushed with frost.

Ruth wrapped her coat tighter as she scanned the pathway that led into the woods. There were broken ferns and a faint indentation in the leaf litter. Something, or someone, had passed this way not long ago. If the members of British Action knew where Clarke was, had one, or several of them, returned to finish the job? Armed officers from the Witness Protection Unit were on their way but she had no idea how long they'd be. Maybe she was just being paranoid? British Action had kidnapped Alfie and now they'd use that as leverage to stop Clarke from testifying. Why risk trying to kill him as well?

As she took a long drag of her cigarette, she longed to be at home with Sarah and Daniel. It had been a long time since she and Sarah had spent a prolonged period of time apart.

The sound of footsteps crunching leaves broke her train of thought. As she turned, she saw Jane approaching. She had a *we need to talk* expression on her face.

'Hey,' Ruth said. 'Caught me.'

Jane laughed. 'You know what, I really did used to smoke behind the bike sheds at school. Me and Tricia Langford. Lambert & Butler.'

'Jesus, that takes me back,' Ruth snorted. 'Me and Sharon Douglas used to smoke Bennies.'

'Benson & Hedges. Classic,' Jane said with a wry smile of recognition.

Ruth nodded back towards the house. 'Any developments?'

'No. They've all gone very quiet,' Jane admitted. 'I think they got their hopes up that Alfie was going to be in that van.'

'We all did,' Ruth said. 'I don't understand where they made the switch. But they seem to be one step ahead of us all the way.'

Jane gave her a dark, significant look. 'There's a leak somewhere, isn't there?'

Ruth nodded and took a breath. 'How else did they know where we were and the code to get in?'

Jane didn't respond for a few seconds and then asked, 'Any suspicions your side?'

'No,' Ruth replied adamantly. 'I've worked with my CID team for years. There's no one that I don't fully trust or they'd be long gone.'

'Of course,' Jane said.

'And no one in my team knew the code for the gates here,' Ruth explained. 'As far as I'm concerned, everything like that is on a need-to-know basis.'

'Agreed,' Jane said deep in thought. 'Who knows this location and the code to the gates? Me, you, Rob? Anyone else?'

'Code is up on the wall,' Ruth pointed out. 'Basically, anyone who has been to the house knows both.'

Ruth wasn't prepared at this stage to flag up that she had some suspicions about Rob. After all, she hardly knew Jane. They could be in it together, although her instinct was that Jane was a good and trustworthy copper.

Jane narrowed her eyes and frowned. 'Family?'

Ruth shrugged. 'Who? I can't believe Ray, Sheila or Chelsie would want Alfie taken. Doesn't make sense. And how? They don't have phones.'

'No,' Jane agreed. 'Unless they didn't know that Alfie was going to be taken.'

Ruth raised an eyebrow. She didn't know what Jane was getting at. 'How do you mean?'

'This might be a stretch,' Jane admitted. 'But we know that Chelsie is desperate not to be here. And she seems to be lurking around every doorway, listening to everything we say.'

Ruth nodded. 'True. You think she might have a phone hidden somewhere?'

'Possibly,' Jane replied. 'And maybe she's let someone know where she is. And even made plans for someone to come and pick her up. As I said, it's a bit of stretch.'

'Yeah, but if not, then we're looking at me, you and Rob,' Ruth said.

'Rob is one of the good guys. Always has been,' Jane said adamantly. 'And me.' She gave a forced smile. 'Well, it's not me.' Then she frowned. 'What about Patricia Hoskins?'

Ruth furrowed her brow. It hadn't crossed her mind but it didn't feel right. 'I've known Patricia for years. I can't see how she'd be involved in any of this.'

Before they could continue, Ruth's phone rang.

It was Nick.

'Boss,' he said.

'Anything from the two suspects you brought back from Stoke?' she asked.

'About to interview them now,' Nick replied. 'The driver of the van is Gary Bentley. We only know that because we've got his photo from Counter Terrorism.'

'What about the others?' she said.

'Nothing,' Nick admitted.

'I've had a call from the Chief Super,' Ruth sighed. 'He's getting it in the neck from the top brass who want to know how we've managed to have a fifteen-year-old boy kidnapped from under our noses and then shoot and kill a member of British Action dead, whether or not it was justifiable.'

Jane signalled to Ruth that she was going to head back into the house.

'Bit of a shitshow all round when you think of the lack of security at Bangor as well,' Nick groaned.

'You're convinced that Darren Nesbitt and the others knew that Bowie's yard was going to be raided?' Ruth asked.

'Not a hundred per cent,' Nick admitted. 'But me and Jade saw them there. We came back two hours later and they'd cleared out. It didn't sit right with me.'

'And we've got a select few people here that knew our whereabouts and the code to the gate,' Ruth said lowering her tone. She didn't want anyone overhearing her so she began to walk towards the edge of the woods. 'Get Jim to do some digging on Jane and Rob. Anything that he thinks is "off". And Patricia Hoskins.'

'Hoskins?' Nick sounded surprised.

'Everyone is a suspect until we rule them out,' Ruth said. 'Were you ringing for a reason to catch me up?'

There was a momentary pause.

'We've had a video through from British Action. It arrived about ten minutes ago,' Nick said in a dark tone. His voice was tight, clipped at the edges like he was holding something back.

Ruth felt her stomach drop. 'Go on,' she said quietly.

'It shows Alfie. And then one of them makes it very clear that unless Clarke retracts all his evidence, refuses to co-operate… they're going to kill Alfie.'

There was a short, stunned silence.

Ruth pinched the bridge of her nose. 'Christ.' She straightened. 'Anything on there we can use to pinpoint a location?'

'Nothing that's obvious,' Nick replied. 'There's a wall behind him but it's just grey breeze blocks. Bit of echo in the audio so it could be a basement or garage. I've already sent it to the Tech boys to clean it up. They might pull something from the background noise. I'll forward it to you now.'

'Okay,' Ruth said. Her voice was flat, but her mind was spinning. 'Even though I'm sure your two suspects will go "no comment" as per usual… keep me posted anyway.'

'Will do.'

Ruth ended the call and exhaled slowly. Her fingers tapped nervously against her phone until a new email pinged into her inbox. There was no subject line. Just an attachment. The video file.

She hesitated for the briefest second, then double-clicked.

Her phone screen lit up. The video was shaky, like it had been filmed on a phone.

It opened on Alfie who was bound to a battered metal chair, wrists tied behind his back, ankles taped to the legs. His face was pale, one eye swollen shut. A strip of gaffer tape was plastered across his mouth. His chest was heaving and he looked like he'd been crying.

Ruth's breath caught in her throat.

Then the camera jolted to the right, revealing a man in a black balaclava, a massive hunting knife clutched in his gloved hand. The blade caught the light. A serrated edge.

'This is a message to you, Ray,' the man growled in his thick Brummie accent. 'If you ever want to see your lad alive again, you know what you've got to do.'

The camera zoomed in slightly, his voice rising.

'Tell those pigs you're not testifying in court. That you don't want to be part of it. That you're done. And you want out, now.'

The lens moved again. Alfie was trembling as the masked man moved behind him, wrapping a hand around Alfie's head, forcing it still. Alfie flinched with a muffled sob escaping under the tape.

The knife slid to his throat and pressed in.

Ruth leaned closer without meaning to, heart hammering.

'Cos if you don't,' the man snarled, 'I'm gonna gut your boy like a pig, and send you his head.'

The video cut off to just black screen. No sound.

Ruth blew out her cheeks, blinking hard. She'd seen some horrible things in her time, but that… that was different.

CHAPTER 37

Nick and Kennedy arrived at Interview Room 2 and stopped outside as Patrick Jefferson opened the door, looking irritated. Jefferson had been instructed by Gary Bentley to act as his solicitor. However, Nick knew full well that Jefferson's services had been requested and paid for by Alexander Hailes, multi-millionaire businessman from Dudley, whom they suspected bankrolled British Action.

Jefferson tapped his watch and gave them a withering look. 'I was rather hoping to get this interview started earlier. I'm keen to get my client home at our earliest convenience.'

Jefferson's public school accent and snotty attitude was getting right up Nick's nose. 'Yeah, well your client isn't going anywhere.'

'We'll see about that,' Jefferson snorted as he gave them a dismissive look while they all walked into the interview room.

Bentley was now dressed in a grey sweatshirt and trackie bottoms. His clothes had been taken for extensive DNA analysis. His mouth had been swabbed for a DNA sample and his nails clipped. His hair was dark and cropped. His beard was short and neat, his eyes blue and steely. The sleeves on his sweatshirt were pushed up to the elbow and revealed thick, muscular forearms that were covered in tattoos, the most prominent being a dagger and the Nazi SS symbol.

Jesus, what a scumbag, Nick thought to himself.

They walked over to the other side of the table and pulled out two chairs.

Bentley then leaned in to talk to Jefferson and whispered something in his ear.

Nick pulled in his chair and looked over at Bentley. His legs were wide open as he slouched in his seat, tattooed hands with fingers laced resting on his stomach. He had a curious smirk on his face as if this was all very amusing. Nick knew the type. Bentley wanted them to know that he wasn't remotely troubled by being arrested.

Kennedy leaned over, took her electronic tablet and made sure that it was turned on.

Jefferson moved a strand of hair from his forehead as he looked over at them. Then he took a page of A4 paper from a folder, put it on the table and turned it so they could take a look. 'Just before we start, my client has already prepared a written statement. In it, he makes it very clear that he had no knowledge of the armed man that was in the back of the van that he was driving. As far as we're concerned, you have no grounds for arresting my client as he hasn't committed any criminal offence. I'd advised him to respond "no comment" to all your questions.' Jefferson gave a patronising shake of his head. 'To save us all the trouble, why don't you just release my client now?'

Nick took a moment, deliberately ignoring the statement and Jefferson's words.

Go and fuck yourself, Nick thought angrily.

The vile image of Alfie, tied up and terrified, came into his mind for a moment. Bentley was involved in that and there was no way he was going to give a scumbag like him an easy ride.

Nick leaned over and pressed the red button on the digital recording equipment. There was a long, loud electronic beep.

'Interview conducted with Gary Bentely, Interview Room 2, Llancastell Police Station. Present are Detective Constable Jade Kennedy, solicitor Robert Jefferson and myself, Detective Sergeant Nick Evans. Time is'—he glanced at the clock on the wall—'three forty-nine p.m.'

Nick then waited a moment before locking eyes with Bentley who continued to wear his faintly amused expression.

'Gary, can you tell us what you know about the kidnapping of Alfie Clarke?' Nick asked.

Bentley narrowed his eyes. 'No comment.'

Nick looked at him. 'Can you tell us where Alfie Clarke is?'

'No comment.'

Nick didn't move and let the silence stretch. Kennedy's pen tapped against her tablet, once. Twice. Then stopped.

Nick leaned forward just a fraction. 'Do you know if he's still alive?'

Bentley gave a single snort of laughter. 'No comment.'

Jefferson shifted in his seat, clearly uncomfortable.

'Because if he's not,' Nick continued, low and level, 'you're not just looking at kidnapping any more. You're looking at murder.'

Bentley scratched his chin, eyes gleaming. He was still and silent.

Nick sat back in frustration. He knew they weren't going to get anything from him and he'd be home that night.

CHAPTER 38

Garrow rubbed a hand over his jaw, his eyes dry from staring at the flickering black-and-white footage for the last hour. He was on the third CCTV video from the Go Local retail park camera – angle six, the one facing the side entrance by the shuttered Greggs.

And there it was.

Three days earlier. Twelve forty-two a.m. The dead of night.

ANPR cameras had picked up the Luton van that had been involved in the armed operation earlier that day.

Garrow watched as the Luton rolled into view, headlights off, engine rumbling low. Same van, same plates. Garrow straightened in his chair as this was interesting.

'Got you,' he muttered.

The van stopped between a skip and a Fiesta. Garrow leaned in, squinting at the screen. A second vehicle, a silver Renault estate, cruised into shot two minutes later, pulling up close. It was too close for a coincidence.

The Renault's driver door opened.

A figure emerged with a hood up, a baseball cap pulled low. They had a slim build, five-six maybe, clad in a dark puffa jacket and jeans. The figure stood still for a beat, scanning the car park, then moved with purpose towards the Luton van.

From the Luton's driver side, Darren Nesbitt stepped out. Even in grainy footage, Garrow recognised his face and that slouched walk. Nesbitt looked over his shoulder, paranoid, his hand buried in his hoodie pocket.

The hooded figure held something – an A4 folder, thick with documents – and something else.

A bundle wrapped in a cloth.

The way they passed it to Nesbitt in a careful, deliberate manner. It was clearly heavy. He held it for a second, then opened the cloth just enough to see the edge of a dark, black shape.

Garrow's breath caught. *Is that a handgun? It has to be the one that Nesbitt used to murder Ashwin Choudary.*

The exchange lasted about thirty seconds.

Nesbitt nodded, then the figure turned and quickly slipped back into the Renault. Both vehicles drove off in opposite directions, their headlights still off.

Garrow pushed away from the screen, his pulse quickening with what he'd discovered.

He needed a second opinion. Turning around, he saw Kennedy returning to her desk. He assumed her and the sarge's interview with Gary Bentley had finished.

'Jade,' Garrow called over. 'I think I've got something.'

'Well, I don't want it,' she joked.

'Very good,' Garrow groaned as he gestured to his computer monitor.

Kennedy strolled over, pulled over a nearby chair and sat down.

'Watch this,' Garrow said.

Kennedy leaned on the desk beside him, hands clasped, watching the footage with intense focus. Her dark curls were tied back in a ponytail.

They watched the whole exchange in silence. When it ended, she frowned.

'Play it again,' she said.

Garrow obliged, dragging the playback to 12:41:58.

Kennedy leaned closer this time, studying the figure in the puffa jacket. When the bundle was handed over, she tapped the screen.

'Stop. There. Zoom.'

Garrow froze the frame. 'You thinking what I'm thinking?'

'That looks like a handgun, yeah,' Kennedy muttered. 'But not just that.'

She pointed to the figure's stance, then rewound again, watching the walk.

'Watch the hips. The body shape. That's a woman.'

Garrow blinked. 'You sure?'

Kennedy nodded, mouth tight. 'She might even be trying to mask it, but it's there. The way she walks. Narrow shoulders, high waist. That's not a bloke.'

'I've looked at all the intel. There aren't any known female members of British Action,' Garrow said. 'That's been consistent across everything we've seen. Every meeting, every march, every raid. It's a boy's club. Pure testosterone and jackboots.'

Kennedy folded her arms. 'Then we've either missed someone… or this woman is under our radar. But she's trusted enough to hand Nesbitt a weapon and confidential documents in the middle of the night.'

'Maybe she's just supplying the gun?' Garrow suggested.

Kennedy didn't look convinced. 'I'm not sure,' she admitted. 'Nesbitt seemed a bit…'

'Deferential?' Garrow said.

'Exactly,' Kennedy agreed. 'And why the folder?'

'What are you thinking?' Garrow asked raising his eyebrow.

Kennedy tapped the screen. 'Maybe this woman is the one calling the shots. We think that it's Neil Baker, Gary Bentley and Steve Bradshaw who run British Action. But maybe this person is the one pulling the strings?'

'We'd better get the digital team to clean that up and see if we can see her face.'

They both stared at the paused screen. Nesbitt's face was just about visible. The woman's features were obscured completely under her cap.

CHAPTER 39

Ruth walked slowly down the gravel driveway of the safe house, her boots crunching the stones with every step. The car had arrived moments ago. It was sleek, black, with windows tinted too dark to see through. Now parked under the skeletal limbs of an old oak, it looked both out of place and utterly necessary.

Two officers from the Witness Protection Unit had emerged, DS Felix Butler and DC Katie Fielding. Felix, in his thirties, had a clipped beard and a face that might've belonged in a magazine if it weren't for the permanent frown etched across his brow. Katie, younger by a few years, had keen eyes and sharp cheekbones.

They'd introduced themselves briskly. There were no handshakes, no small talk. Now they were doing a sweep of the grounds, eyes flitting from shadows to windows, shoulders tense. Ruth had noticed the Glock 17s holstered on their hips. Normally the sight of firearms unsettled her. Today, they were oddly comforting. If British Action came back, they'd meet stern resistance.

Felix strode back from the security gates, tugging the collar of his fitted black jacket higher against the cold. 'Everything looks in order, ma'am,' he said. His accent was unmistakably middle-class and well educated. Ruth guessed boarding school. Oxford or maybe Durham.

'Thank you,' she said, managing a tired smile.

He nodded towards the gates. 'I take it the code hasn't been changed since the kidnapping incident?'

Ruth winced slightly. 'We were hoping you could handle that. None of us have touched it. There's too much going on.'

'No problem,' Felix replied. 'I'll reset it now, then sit down with the family and outline how we're going to proceed.'

Ruth hesitated. His tone was firm and authoritative. It almost sounded like they were taking over. Usually in this type of situation, that's exactly what would be happening now. The Clarke family were now in protective custody under the UK's Witness Protection Unit. But things were developing rapidly so that it wasn't as clear-cut as that.

She cleared her throat. 'We haven't shown them the video yet. Of Alfie.'

Felix's eyes flicked to hers. 'Why not?'

'I told them it would be too upsetting. But Ray's cracking. He's talking about retracting his statement. I understand why. He thinks if he backs out and they get Alfie back, they can just go home and be left alone.'

'Which they won't be,' Felix said quietly. 'They won't trust him ever again.'

'No,' Ruth agreed, voice brittle. 'We've made that very clear. And Sheila isn't helping. In fact, she's pressuring him to walk away. But maybe... maybe hearing it from someone new might help.'

'I'll speak to them both,' Felix said confidently. 'Assess what we're working with.'

'Thanks,' Ruth said, and meant it. She watched him walk away, purposeful and precise, his boots grinding noisily on the gravel and leaves. She only hoped it wasn't already too late.

As she reached for a cigarette, Ruth's mind was whirring. Thinking about poor Alfie and where he was being kept. The concern that someone was leaking information about the investigation to British Action. And the whereabouts of Darren Nesbitt. Talk about keeping plates spinning.

Ruth clicked her lighter but stopped.

She could hear raised voices from somewhere.

What's that?

Or was it just one raised voice?

Where's that coming from?

The wind stirred, sharp with the odour of lake below. Putting the cigarette and lighter back into her pocket, Ruth slowly followed the direction of the sound, heart starting to thump.

It sounded like someone was in the woods.

Entering, the thick autumnal leaves swished beneath her feet, damp and mulching from recent rain.

Getting closer, Ruth could hear that it was a woman's voice. Angry. Urgent.

She stopped and strained her hearing.

And then she recognised it.

It was Chelsie.

And she was having a blazing row with someone on a *phone*. Which should be impossible as Chelsie had handed both her phone and laptop to police officers.

Ruth came into a clearing and saw that Chelsie was holding a small black 'burner' phone to her ear.

You've got to be bloody kidding me!

Oblivious to Ruth's presence, Chelsie continued her heated conversation for a few more seconds.

Then Chelsie became aware of Ruth's presence.

'Oh, shit. I've got to go,' she hissed into the phone as she took the phone from her ear and looked defiantly at Ruth.

Ruth shook her head. 'Who were you talking to, Chelsie?'

'I don't think that's any of your business, is it?' she replied but she was clearly rattled.

'You were instructed to hand over your phone, laptop and any other digital devices to my officers,' Ruth snapped sternly. 'So, who were you talking to?'

Chelsie shrugged but she was starting to lose her brash exterior. 'My boyfriend. That's all.'

'What's his name?' Ruth demanded.

'Ben,' Chelsie mumbled.

Ruth raised an eyebrow.

'Ben Underwood,' she sighed.

'Did you tell him where you are?' Ruth said.

'No. No of course not!' Chelsie insisted with a frown. 'I'm not stupid.'

Her response seemed genuine enough. But someone had revealed their location and the code to the security gates. Maybe the leak was as simple as Chelsie talking to someone back home? Had someone – her boyfriend – offered to come and get her and Chelsie had simply gave out the location and code? Ruth knew how desperate Chelsie was to get back home to see her friends.

'I'm going to need you to think very carefully when you answer this question, Chelsie,' Ruth said deliberately. 'Have you told anyone where you and your family are staying at the moment?'

Chelsie hesitated. 'No,' she said. Ruth wasn't sure that she was telling her the truth.

'Are you sure about that?' Ruth asked, searching Chelsie's face for the telltale signs that she wasn't being truthful. It was very hard to tell, which was unusual.

'Yes. I haven't told anyone anything,' Chelsie insisted. 'I'm not an idiot.'

Ruth held out her hand. There was one way of checking who Chelsie had been talking to. 'Give me your phone please.'

'What?' Chelsie said with a suspicious look.

'I'm going to need to have your phone,' Ruth said sternly and gave her a look to show that she meant it.

Chelsie gave a withering sigh and she took two steps forward and handed Ruth the burner phone.

With a quick check, Ruth scrolled through the calls that Chelsie had made since arriving at the safe house. There were about a dozen. But with a quick look, it seemed that Chelsie had only called three different numbers.

Ruth then gestured back towards the safe house. 'Come on,' Ruth said in a quieter voice. 'When we get back, I'm going to need you to tell me everyone you've called and exactly what you've told them.'

Chelsie gave a little nod. The surly attitude had gone now and had been replaced by an awkward sheepishness.

CHAPTER 40

Nick sat dressed in his thick navy dressing gown gazing at his laptop in the small room that served as a study in his house. It had just gone four a.m. He'd come home from CID, showered, had some food and grabbed just over three hours sleep. Over the years, he'd become fairly used to getting this little sleep when working on a major homicide investigation.

The study was quiet and still. A small desk lamp cast a soft vanilla glow across the room. Nick had the slatted blinds open to keep an eye on the road outside. With a quick click, Nick logged onto the software that was linked to his doorbell video. Then he clicked onto the video folder that covered the past seven hours.

Trawling through the footage at high speed, he saw something at two thirteen a.m. that caught his eye. Stopping the video, he peered at the scene. His heart sank. The car that he'd spotted sitting outside the house before, was parked up again. The camera was too far to see the figure sitting inside.

Who the hell is that? he wondered with a mixture of frustration and fear.

'Couldn't sleep?' said a sleepy voice.

Amanda came into the room looking bleary eyed and yawned.

Closing the laptop as surreptitiously as he could, Nick gave her smile. He didn't want to scare her unduly until he knew who it was that kept parking up outside their home.

'No,' Nick sighed as he stood up, took her in his arms and gave her a kiss.

'I'm glad that you brushed your teeth when you got up,' Amanda said deadpan as she looked at him.

Nick frowned. 'I didn't.'

'No, I know,' she replied with wry smile. 'But maybe you should. Possibly with bleach.'

'Hey!' Nick pulled back, wounded. 'It's not *that* bad.'

'Nick, love of my life, father of our child, wielder of the dragon breath – it's terrible. Like a chemical weapon. There's some gargle in the bathroom.'

Nick gave her a dry, amused look. 'And they say romance is dead.'

Amanda kissed his forehead. 'Right, I'm going back to bed. Love you.'

'Love you too,' Nick said.

'You coming back in?'

Nick shook his head. 'I've gotta go back in.'

'No sign of that poor boy yet?'

Nick shook his head. 'Not yet. But we'll find him.'

Amanda nodded and then left, pulling the door to.

His mobile phone rang. It was Ruth.

'Boss,' he said answering.

'Nick. Where are you?' she asked sleepily.

'Home. I'm about to head back in,' Nick explained.

'I tried you earlier,' Ruth said casually. 'I caught Clarke's daughter with a burner phone.'

'What?'

'She reckons that she's only been ringing her boyfriend,' Ruth explained. 'Ben Underwood. Nothing on the PNC. Plus, a couple of other friends who check out. But I need you to cross-check the numbers in case she's lying to us.'

'No problem You think she's the one that revealed your location,' Nick asked as he tried to process what Ruth had told him.

'I'm not sure,' Ruth admitted. 'There is a chance that she's told the boyfriend where she is and the code to get in so that he'll come and get her. And somehow that information has found its way into the hands of British Action.'

'Doesn't explain how they knew we were going to raid Bowie's scrapyard,' Nick said.

'No, it doesn't,' Ruth agreed. 'And maybe she's actually telling us the truth.'

'Do you think she is?' Nick asked.

'Not sure,' Ruth replied. 'I can't get a proper read on her. She's good at doing the whole stroppy teenager thing but I suspect there's more to her than that.'

'What about Clarke?'

'He's on the verge of leaving,' Ruth admitted. 'Unless we can find Alfie in the next few hours, I think he'll walk.'

CHAPTER 41

Ruth blinked and gazed up at the ceiling. A faint throb pressed behind her eyes, the kind that came from a night of broken sleep and too much thinking. She reached for her phone on the small table beside the bed and squinted at the screen. Five thirty a.m.

It was too early. But she knew sleep wouldn't be returning.

The farmhouse around her groaned. She could hear the wind brushing softly against the gable end, and the occasional creak in the ceiling.

She checked her messages. A few exchanges with Sarah from last night. Daniel had decided he wanted to be a goalkeeper and had asked for gloves, apparently with great seriousness. Ruth smiled despite herself. In the middle of the chaos the Clarkes were living through, Sarah had somehow kept their adopted son's world stitched together. A tight-knit family, she thought, not for the first time, with a pang of fierce gratitude. Whatever happened today, she had that.

She threw back the duvet. The room smelled of damp wood. The house had been updated. MI5 had made it secure enough to monitor the perimeter, but it was still a nineteenth-century farmhouse.

Her mind swung straight to Alfie. She prayed that today would be the day they found him. The image of him, small and terrified, hidden away in some godforsaken place was too much to hold for long. Her chest felt tight.

Coffee. And a cigarette. That's what I need.

Ruth pulled on her trainers, tugged on her joggers and hoodie, then stepped into the corridor. The air was cold and biting. The small sash windows lining the landing were fogged up with condensation. She paused at one and wiped a sleeve across the glass, peering out. The sky was a dull charcoal grey, the trees looming, their leaves heavy and unmoving. The surrounding fields were swallowed in mist. Nothing stirred.

The house made another groaning noise. A floorboard somewhere deep in the structure shifted with a slow, wooden sigh.

As she descended the stairs, each step gave a quiet creak under her weight. It was subtle, but in the silence of the house, every sound became exaggerated. The banister was smooth and cold beneath her fingers.

The smell of coffee reached her before she hit the bottom step. Rich and slightly burnt. Someone was already up. It had to be Felix, the Witness Protection Officer. He'd told her he'd stay downstairs through the night.

She moved quietly across the flagstone hallway and into the kitchen, where a pot of coffee sat on the hot plate, steam curling up in lazy spirals. She poured herself a mug, strong, black, and sipped it carefully. *Perfect.* The heat was a welcome jolt.

From the hallway, she heard a low shuffle and followed it into the living room. Felix was there, lounging on the edge of the sofa, scrolling on his phone. He looked surprisingly fresh.

'Morning,' he said without looking up, then offered a small nod as their eyes met. His supreme confidence was impressive. But Ruth wondered what was really going on behind that assured certainty.

'Everything okay last night?' Ruth asked, her voice a little hoarse.

'Not a peep,' he said with a shrug. 'Quiet as a grave.'

Ruth raised an eyebrow. 'Let's hope it stays that way.' She gestured towards the front door with her mug. 'I'm going to get some fresh air.'

Felix gave a knowing look, a smile flickering. 'Ah, right. DCI Murphy went out about ten minutes ago.'

Ruth returned the smile. She turned and made her way back down the narrow hallway, her footsteps soft against the worn wooden floor.

She opened the heavy front door.

Outside, over to the east, the sky was beginning to soften with the first flush of light, but the woods were still a dark mass, looming and impenetrable.

She stepped out slowly. Her eyes adjusted to the gloom. Somewhere far off, a bird gave a hesitant chirrup, then fell silent again.

That's when she heard it. A low, indistinct murmuring. Male. Not close, but not far either. She stilled her breath and strained to listen.

There was a voice. Down near the edge of the woods, just where the trees began to blur into shadow. Just like yesterday except it was a man's voice this time.

She moved quietly to the edge of the stone steps, feet careful on the wet surface.

It was Rob.

He stood half-obscured by the mist and the edge of the treeline, phone pressed to his ear. He was pacing, just a little. His shoulders were tight, his movements erratic. He gestured once, sharply, and ran his hand through his hair. The phone was clutched close to his mouth.

Ruth remained frozen, eyes fixed on him. Something about his posture, his presence was 'off'. Not obviously wrong. But his body language and facial expressions were ones of concern, even fear.

She took a slow step forward and her trainers squeaked on the wet stone.

Rob's head twitched and then turned.

He saw her.

His face changed instantly. First he looked surprised, then something else. Something darker. Guilt? Panic? It flitted across his features like a shadow and was gone. But she'd seen it. She knew she had.

His mouth opened slightly, but no sound came. Then it shut again.

They stared at each other for a beat too long.

Ruth moved down the steps, coffee still warm in her hand, the ceramic mug heating her fingers. Her expression was neutral, but inside her mind was turning over at speed.

Rob ended the call far too quickly. A single jab at the screen which was abrupt and final. He gave her a smile which was too quick, too wide. It didn't touch his eyes. He gave a casual wave, a half-hearted gesture of normality.

There is definitely something wrong here.

She didn't return the wave.

Instead, she took another slow sip of her coffee and crossed the final step, her pace measured.

The silence hung heavy again.

'Morning,' she said eventually. Her voice was calm, even warm on the surface.

Rob smiled again. 'Morning.' Then he shifted gears to break the tension. 'Anything on Alfie yet?'

Ruth shook her head, releasing a breath that was more frustration than air. 'Nothing.'

But she was lying now. Not outright, but by omission. She could no longer afford to be open with him. If Rob was the leak – and her gut was increasingly refusing to rule it out – then every word she gave him could work against them. It was like a game of chess played blindfolded, every move shadowed in mistrust.

'Jesus,' Rob muttered, running a hand through his hair again. He gestured vaguely back at the house. 'If we don't find him this morning, they're all going to walk.'

Ruth took her time replying. 'We've got every officer in North Wales, Staffordshire and Cheshire looking for Alfie. Someone's going to crack. We just need a break.'

Rob nodded, though the movement was tight. 'What time's your DS doing the press conference?'

'Nine,' Ruth replied, glancing at her watch. 'We're hoping going public will jog someone's memory. A sighting, anything. Plus, it's a bit of damage control as the media are hammering us.'

Rob nodded again, then looked at her more directly. 'You got any closer to working out who's been leaking to British Action?'

Ruth's eyes narrowed just slightly.

Funny that he'd mention them now. It was almost too casually dropped in.

She offered a half-shrug. 'Thought it might've been Chelsie. But the numbers on her phone all check out. And she just... doesn't have the clout to get hold of gate codes or raid intel. It can't be her.'

'Which means it's someone high up,' Rob said.

'Yes.' She let the word hang.

He studied her. 'You're starting to wonder about Jane and me?'

Ruth laughed softly. Dismissive. 'No. Of course not.'

'I wouldn't blame you,' he said. 'I know my politics are a bit right of centre. But British Action? I think the *Daily Mail* is too far right. That's how far off I am.'

Well, you would say that, wouldn't you?

She didn't respond. Just watched him. Studied his every flicker and every breath.

'Boss?'

The voice cut through the tension like a blade. Jane.

She was striding towards them from the house, jacket thrown over one shoulder, her face taut with something that looked very much like alarm.

Rob straightened instinctively.

'Everything all right?' he asked, voice clipped.

Jane reached them, her cheeks flushed from the cold.

'We've got another video,' she said. 'From British Action.'

CHAPTER 42

Nick scanned the faces in the packed press room, the heavy camera lights already making the room feel hot and his shirt cling beneath the arms. The large image of Alfie Clarke, fifteen years old, stared down from behind him. A school photo, crooked tie and a hesitant smile. Seeing it that size made Alfie look even younger.

He leaned into the mic and cleared his throat.

'Good morning. I'm Detective Sergeant Nick Evans of North Wales Police. I'm here to appeal for information regarding the disappearance of Alfie Clarke, who we now believe has been kidnapped.'

The room hushed and murmurs died quickly.

'We believe Alfie may be being held against his will somewhere in the Stoke-on-Trent area. Evidence gathered in the last twenty-four hours suggests a possible connection to the far-right terrorist organisation known as British Action.'

A ripple moved across the press pack. There were a couple of glances exchanged.

Nick continued, his voice steady, but his fingers were clenched beneath the table. He hated public speaking. 'This group is proscribed. They are dangerous. We're asking anyone who has seen Alfie, knows of his whereabouts, or may have witnessed any suspicious activity in or around the Stoke area to come forward immediately. You can do so anonymously. No detail is too small.'

From her place beside him, Kerry Mahoney, the press officer for North Wales Police, sat still, lips pressed tight with a faintly smug satisfaction. Nick could already feel her watching and judging him. She was probably clocking every misplaced pause. On the few occasions that he'd encountered her, she'd always had that disapproving headmistress air. Even now, she gave a little cough as if cueing him to wind up.

Nick ignored her. *Snotty cow.*

'I'll take a few questions,' he said just to spite her.

A journalist in a navy suit shot up a hand. 'Sergeant Evans, are you confirming that British Action is behind Alfie Clarke's kidnapping?'

'We're not confirming it. But it is one of the lines of inquiry we are pursuing,' Nick said in a steady voice.

A buzz of whispers.

Another reporter piped up, his voice sharp. 'Do you believe Alfie's life is in immediate danger?'

Nick hesitated a fraction too long.

'Yes,' he admitted. 'We do believe that his life is in danger and that's why we need to find him as soon as possible. And that's why we are appealing to the public for help.'

Mahoney shifted in her seat again, adjusting the mic like she was ready to jump in. She always had a knack for making it clear she thought she could do a better job.

Nick caught the movement and added quickly, 'Please, if you have any information, anything at all, contact the numbers listed behind me. We are treating this as a live and urgent case. Time is critical.'

'Is there any CCTV footage?' someone shouted from the back.

'We're reviewing several hours of footage,' Nick replied. 'But as of now, there's nothing we can release publicly.'

Another journalist, older, leaned forward. 'Why isn't this being led by the Counter Terrorism Unit if there's a suspected link to a terror group?'

Nick exhaled slowly. 'This is a joint operation between North Wales Police and Special Crime and Counter Terrorism Division. They are fully involved and we are working collaboratively.'

Mahoney was reaching for her mic now. Nick nodded curtly and moved back from the table. He was happy to wind things up now as the questions were getting tricky.

'Thank you, that's all for now,' she said with a rehearsed smile that didn't reach her eyes. 'We'll provide updates as soon as we're able.'

Nick gathered his notes and turned to leave. As he passed Mahoney, she gave him a tight little smile. She probably thought she'd just bailed him out. She always did enjoy swooping in.

As he went out, Nick clocked the large photo of Alfie's face. *Come on, Alfie. Where the hell are you?*

CHAPTER 43

The office in the safe house smelled of coffee. A single lamp threw dull light across the metal desk, where Ruth sat with Rob and Jane. The laptop screen glowed in front of them, the cursor blinking over the file name.

Rob reached forward and clicked.

The video opened immediately. It was low-resolution, the grainy telltale of a mobile phone. The screen shook, tilted, then steadied.

Ruth took a breath as she watched intently.

Alfie appeared on the screen.

As they'd seen in the other video, he was bound to a steel chair and looked barely conscious. His skinny frame sagged against the restraints, his wrists tied behind him, legs bound tight to the chair's legs with silver duct tape. A strip of gaffer tape sealed his mouth, but even through that, they could hear the sobs.

Ruth felt her stomach drop. A sickening dread rose in her chest.

'Jesus Christ,' Jane whispered.

Alfie's head lolled, his fringe stuck to his forehead with sweat. His right eye was swollen shut. There was bruising across his cheek.

The camera jolted, then the same man as before stepped into frame. He was dressed in black from head to toe. Tactical gloves, combat trousers, and a tight-fitting black hoodie. But it was the balaclava that made Ruth's skin crawl. That, and the hunting knife he held in one gloved hand. It was long and serrated.

'We're getting fed up waiting for you, Ray. So, this is a new message for you,' the masked man said, his voice thick with a Birmingham accent.

The camera zoomed in slightly. Ruth could see the gleam of the blade under harsh artificial light. The man's stance was military and his grip was firm.

'You've got until two o'clock. That's your deadline. Two o'clock today, Ray. You tell the police, the CPS, everyone, that you're out. That you're not going to trial. That you're not giving evidence.'

He paused.

'Because if you don't...'

He stepped behind Alfie. The boy froze, body taut with fear. The man grabbed Alfie's right hand and forced it down onto the tabletop.

Alfie moaned behind the tape, his eyes wide with terror.

The man pushed Alfie's hand down hard, spreading out his fingers. Then he took the knife's blade and pushed it hard into Alfie's forefinger.

Ruth held her breath. *Please God, don't...*

'We start cutting them off,' the man said. 'One finger. Every hour after two o'clock. You hear me, Ray? At three, it's one. At four, it's two. We'll keep going until he's got nothing left but stumps. Or until you get the message to us and do what needs doing.'

Ruth could feel her heart thundering. Jane had gone pale, her mouth clamped shut. Rob leaned forward, his fists clenched.

'You've been warned, Ray. You're a fucking grass. So, it's time to make your mind up about what you want to do.'

The video ended.

There was a horrible silence.

The room remained frozen in the glow of the laptop.

Ruth sat back slowly, exhaling through her nose and shaking her head.

'Jesus,' Rob whispered.

Before anyone could respond any more, the door burst open.

'Sheila!' Ruth looked over but it was too late.

Sheila stood in the doorway, her face drained of colour. Her eyes locked on the laptop screen and the image of Alfie.

She'd heard enough.

'That was Alfie,' she murmured, stepping forward.

'Sheila, don't.' Ruth stood to block the screen, but Sheila pushed past.

'I heard it. They're going to hurt him. They're going to...' she said hoarsely. Her eyes were wide with utter disbelief, as if seeing her stepson like that hadn't quite landed in her brain yet. 'They're going to cut his fingers off. I heard that man say it.'

Ruth's voice was calm and low. 'We're doing everything we can. Please, just take a step back. Let us…'

But Sheila was already backing out of the room. 'Ray! RAY!' she yelled.

He appeared a moment later looking anxious and confused. 'What is it? What's happened?'

'It's Alfie,' she said, her voice breaking with emotion. 'Those bastards sent a video. They said they'll hurt him, cut him, Ray. Unless you back out. Unless you say you won't testify.'

Ray stared at her in horror. 'They said that?'

'They said two o'clock. They're going to start with his fingers.' She was crying now, properly crying. Putting her hand to her face. 'Every hour.'

Ray turned to the officers and narrowed his eyes. 'Is that right?'

Ruth nodded.

'I'm out,' Ray said instantly. 'That's it. I'm done.'

'Ray…' Jane started.

'No. No, I mean it. I don't care what deals you've made or what witness protection means. I'm not risking my boy for this. No chance.' He turned to Sheila. 'Go get our stuff. Get Chelsie and Alfie's things. We're leaving.'

'You can't just walk away,' Ruth said. Her tone was controlled, but firm. 'Even if you do this, if you pull out, there are no guarantees that you're going to get Alfie back safely. You've only got their word for it.'

'That's a chance I'll take,' Ray snapped. 'I'll do anything to get him back. And you'd do the same if you were me.'

Ruth took a step forward. 'Ray, I know how hard this is…'

'You don't!' Ray said, interrupting her. 'You don't know what it's like to see your kid like that and know it's because of you. I'm not going to be the reason they send him back to us in bits.'

'Ray, please,' Jane tried. 'I don't think you're going to be safe going back home. With no protection.'

'I don't care about that. I want to take everything back. Every word I ever said about British Action. I want it off the record. And I want them to know that I've done it. I want them to see I've done what they asked.'

Sheila was already gone, back to the bedrooms. Ruth could hear her shouting for Chelsie.

'Ray,' Rob said, trying a softer tone. 'If you back out now, the entire operation...'

'I've made my mind up.' He turned on his heel and walked out.

The door slammed behind him.

Silence.

Ruth stared at the blank screen. 'We've got to find Alfie,' she said quietly.

CHAPTER 44

'Right, listen up, everyone,' Nick said as he strode to the front of the CID office, his voice taut with urgency. His jaw was clenched, eyes bloodshot from lack of sleep. The CID team were already assembled, the air thick with the mingled smells of burnt bacon from the downstairs cafe, strong coffee and male sweat. An edge of tension buzzed under the fluorescent strip lights. They were all running on caffeine and adrenaline. 'Ray Clarke is retracting his statement and refusing to testify at trial against the leaders of British Action. We've just received another video from British Action. Alfie's in it.'

A frustrated murmur passed through the room.

'They're threatening to chop off one of Alfie's fingers for every hour after two p.m. that Clarke doesn't withdraw his evidence. I guess the pressure got too much for him.'

There was a pause as the words settled. Someone swore quietly.

'I've asked the Tech boys to clean the video up to see if there's anything in the background, noise, maybe a reflection that gives us a clue where Alfie's being held. But I'm not holding my breath.' Nick's face was grim. 'So, unless we can find and rescue Alfie this morning, the whole case is going to collapse. And with it, any chance of putting British Action away.'

The team shifted uneasily.

'Sarge,' Garrow said, raising his hand. He gestured to his monitor. 'I think I've got something. CCTV footage from a rural bus route. Bickerton Road, heading out of Wrexham towards Shropshire and Stoke.'

'Let's see it,' Nick said, moving to the side to make room at the wall-mounted monitor. The screen flickered, then burst into life. A dashcam view from the front of the bus played. Rolling green hills and hedgerows blurred past the windscreen.

'Here,' Garrow narrated, pointing. 'We're heading up through Bickerton. And just there on the left. Can you see that? A lay-by with a burger van. And parked next to it.' He paused the footage, got up, and walked to the screen. He stabbed his finger at the paused frame. 'That's the Luton van. Same one from yesterday. The one we cornered in the retail park in Stoke. Bowie's scrapyard details are clearly on the back.'

Nick leaned in and squinted.

'And right behind it...' Garrow zoomed in slightly. 'That's a silver VW Golf. Passenger door open. Rear doors too. Looks like someone's being moved, quickly.'

Nick's heart rate kicked up a notch. 'This is where they made the switch. Alfie was moved from the van to the Golf.'

'Can we make out the plate?' Kennedy asked from behind her desk.

Nick narrowed his eyes, peering at the grainy image. 'Just about. Someone write this down: yankee-zebra-one-nine, tango-oscar-sierra.'

Garrow was already typing. 'Calling the DVLA now,' he said as his fingers flew across the keyboard.

'Anything else?' Nick asked, turning back to the room.

Kennedy leaned forward, her tone more measured but no less urgent. 'Bit of a strange one, Sarge. The boss asked me to dig into Patricia Hoskins. The CPS lawyer.'

Nick looked puzzled. 'Hoskins?'

Kennedy nodded. 'Yeah. Long shot, I know. But she had access, knew about the raid on Bowie's yard, knew the safe house location and code. If there's a leak, she could be it.'

Nick gave her a sceptical look. He and Ruth had worked with Hoskins on at least half a dozen cases with no issues. She was a very good lawyer.

Kennedy tapped her keyboard and brought up an image on the wall monitor. 'This was taken about eighteen months ago at a Law Society Ball in Chester.'

The image filled the screen. Patricia Hoskins was wearing an elegant navy evening gown, one hand holding a tall flute of champagne, the other resting casually on the arm of a distinguished, silver-haired man in his seventies. He wore a dinner suit and bow tie and was clearly mid-laugh, her eyes fixed on Hoskins.

'That's Alexander Hailes,' Nick said, frowning and thrown by what he could see.

Hailes. The elusive millionaire businessman long suspected of secretly funding British Action. Always one step ahead of financial investigators. Always denying involvement.

'What the hell is she doing with him?' Kennedy asked, narrowing her eyes.

Nick didn't answer right away. The question hung in the air.

'Is she the leak?' she asked softly, more to herself than anyone.

Nick exhaled, slow and hard. 'Someone's been feeding British Action. That much is clear. And Patricia Hoskins looks very comfortable on the arm of the man who bankrolls them.' He jabbed a finger at the photo. 'I'll talk to the boss. But we may need to pull her in.'

Before anyone could respond, Garrow shot upright from his desk.

'Got it!' he said, voice cracking slightly. 'The VW Golf's registered to a Wendy Palmer. Lives in Stoke-on-Trent. I've got the address here.' He walked quickly across the office and handed Nick a Post-it note.

Nick took it, scanned the details, then locked eyes with Kennedy. 'Get your coat.'

As they swept out of the office, the tension didn't break. It tightened. The clock was ticking. And somewhere, a terrified teenager was running out of time.

CHAPTER 45

Ruth grabbed her third mug of coffee for the day, came out of the safe house kitchen and headed down the hallway. She spotted something out of the corner of her eye. Sheila was coming slowly down the staircase, suitcase in each hand. Their eyes met for a second.

'I'm sorry it's come to this,' Ruth said quietly.

'So am I,' Sheila said in a virtual whisper. Then she gave Ruth a searching look. 'Is there any news about Alfie?' she asked, the distress etched deep into her face. Even though Sheila was Alfie's stepmother and had only been part of the Clarke family for a couple of years, her love and concern for Alfie was clearly overwhelming.

'No. I'm sorry,' Ruth admitted. 'But I promise you, we're going to find him and bring him back to you safely.'

Sheila gave her a blank look as she got to the foot of the stairs and walked over to put the suitcases down. 'You don't know that,' she sighed. 'Those men are bastards. They're animals.'

Ruth gave her a supportive look. 'I'm going to ring my team now. And I'll let you know the minute I hear anything.'

Sheila gave a little shrug. Ruth's words had made no impact on her anxiety or her ability to trust her or her officers.

With a little sigh, Ruth made her way towards the front door that was open by about six inches and went outside.

Over by where the cars were parked, Rob, Jane and Felix were having a conversation. Arrangements needed to be made to take Ray, Sheila and Chelsie back to their home in Stoke. Felix kept glancing over his shoulder.

Ruth also knew she had the unenviable task of contacting British Action. She'd have to confirm that Clarke had withdrawn all evidence, would not testify in court, and was refusing to co-operate in any way.

She glanced towards Bala Lake. A breeze blew sharply off the water, carrying with it the smell of damp earth and distant pine. The lake's surface had now darkened to pewter. In the distance, ink-black clouds were spreading their canopy over the ridges of the Snowdonia mountains, swallowing light with unnerving speed. A storm was coming. Ruth could feel it in her bones. Somewhere behind the trees, a lone crow cawed once, then fell silent.

It felt tense and ominous. Too quiet. Too still.

The tension was broken as her phone rang. It was Nick.

'Boss,' he said with a sense of urgency.

'Nick?'

'We've got bus dashcam footage which shows that Alfie was transferred from that Luton van to a silver VW Golf en route,' Nick explained.

'Can you see the registration?' she asked, hoping that this was going to be the lead that they needed.

'Yes. The registered address is in Stoke,' Nick continued. 'We're heading to the address now. I've got an Armed Response Unit on standby.'

'Good,' Ruth said as her pulse quickened. 'Keep me posted.'

'Will do. Something else,' he said.

'What's that?'

'Jim is going to send you over a photo now,' Nick said. 'Patricia Hoskins at some swanky law ball. And she's looking very cosy with Alexander Hailes.'

'What?' Ruth virtually spat out the word. 'You're bloody joking!'

'I wish I was,' Nick admitted.

'Leave it with me,' Ruth said. 'And you and Jade be careful when you arrive. No bloody heroics.'

'No problem,' Nick said as he ended the call.

CHAPTER 46

Ten minutes later, Ruth wrapped the fingers of her right hand around a hot mug of tea. In her left hand, she was holding her phone. She was wondering how long it would be before Nick and Kennedy arrived at the address in Stoke. She could feel the tension in her stomach. She glanced at the time on her phone. Twelve thirty-five p.m. The time seemed to be racing towards two p.m.

Then she clicked back on the photo that Garrow had sent over. Patricia Hoskins casually on the arm of Alexander Hailes. Both laughing.

How the hell is that possible? Ruth thought to herself. She'd always had Patricia Hoskins down as a completely trustworthy, scrupulous CPS lawyer. Yet here she was fraternising with a man who was rumoured to be bankrolling far-right terrorists. Hoskins wasn't naïve enough not to have heard those rumours. And by the looks of the photo, it had been taken in the past year or two. *What was she thinking?*

And then, of course, a much darker thought. Was Hoskins the leak? She had access to all the classified information that someone had passed on to British Action. And here she was, clearly very close to a scumbag like Hailes. It had to be her that leaked the details, didn't it?

The first thing Ruth needed to do was to make sure no more information was passed to Hoskins. And then she needed to flag up her suspicions. Or did she need to confront Hoskins with what she knew? See what she had to say for herself.

Ruth scrolled through her phone looking for Hoskins's number. She would find some reason why she needed to talk. Some small procedural query to keep things on the level. Nothing confrontational. She tapped the screen and brought the phone to her ear.

There were three rings and then her voicemail.

'This is Patricia Hoskins. I'm away from the office for the next two weeks. Please direct all urgent queries to the CPS North Wales main line. Thank you.'

Ruth pulled the phone away slowly.

Two weeks? That made no sense. They were mid-case, for God's sake. Hoskins had insisted on being the point of contact for every statement, every piece of new evidence.

What the hell is going on?

Ruth sat up straighter as she tapped out the CPS's main number and waited. The call was answered quickly. A clipped, polite female voice that Ruth didn't recognise.

'Crown Prosecution Service, North Wales. How can I help?' asked the woman.

'Yes, Detective Inspector Ruth Hunter. I've been working with Patricia Hoskins. I've just tried her line and got her voicemail. She says she's away for two weeks. Can you tell me what's going on?'

'One moment, please.'

There was the rustle of a keyboard, the sound of paper being moved and then the voice returned.

'Ms Hoskins is currently on leave due to personal reasons. Another member of the CPS team is taking over her cases, and they'll be in contact with you by the end of the day.'

Ruth stared out the window, eyes narrowing as the words sank in.

'Who's replacing her?' Ruth asked. She knew several of the North Wales CPS lawyers.

'I'm afraid I can't give that name out yet. The allocation is still being finalised.'

'Right. Thank you.' Ruth ended the call, feeling confused and then sat in silence.

Personal reasons? What does that even mean? A CPS lawyer like Hoskins didn't take time off. Not during a major investigation. Not unless something was very wrong. Or did she have something to hide.

Ruth got to her feet and paced the kitchen. The floorboard beneath the far window creaked as she looked at the photo again. Hoskins laughing with Hailes, who'd made his fortune in property speculation and laundered it through shell charities that financed violence and fear. They looked relaxed and way too familiar.

Was it simply old friends, old ties? Or something more? A slip in judgement or complete betrayal.

Outside, the light was starting to thin. The kind of washed-out, colourless afternoon light that reminded Ruth of her first winter in Snowdonia. The time she'd thought the isolation might undo her completely. It was a time when Ruth wondered what the hell she'd done coming all the way from South London to North Wales.

She pressed her hand against the cold glass of the window, staring out at the tangled branches beyond. Hoskins had always struck her as sharp, proper. One of the good ones. The kind you could trust to cross every 't' and dot every 'i', to never let her personal life bleed into the job. But now Ruth wasn't sure.

The door creaked behind her. It was Jane. She had a concerned look on her face.

'Everything all right?' Ruth asked her.

Jane shook her head. 'They're all packing up the rest of their stuff upstairs. Any word from your guys and that address in Stoke?'

'Not yet,' Ruth admitted.

'What has Patricia Hoskins had to say about this?' Jane asked.

Ruth took a few seconds. Was she going to reveal her suspicions about Hoskins to Jane? Or wait. Ruth was finding it hard to know who to trust. But her instinct was that Hoskins was involved somewhere along the line. How else could they explain her erratic behaviour?

Ruth pulled a face as she turned the screen. 'Yeah, there's something I need to show you.'

Jane came over to look at the photo on Ruth's phone. 'Oh, my God,' she whispered. Then she took another look as if she couldn't quite believe what she was seeing.

'I know,' Ruth sighed. 'I've tried to get hold of her. But the CPS are telling me that she's away for two weeks for personal reasons.'

Jane narrowed her eyes. 'You think she's the leak?'

Ruth shrugged. 'She has to be, doesn't she?'

'I guess. And if I could find her, I'd arrest her,' Ruth said angrily.

Jane frowned. 'We've had two attempts to hack into the Counter Terrorism Division server,' she explained. 'I wonder if that's connected.'

'Maybe.'

Jane gestured to the door. 'I'd better go and tell Rob.'

Ruth didn't like to tell her that until about ten minutes ago, her suspicions were all focused on Rob.

'I'll let you know as soon as my officers get to that address,' Ruth said.

'Great,' Jane said as she turned and left the room.

Outside, the wind was rising, rattling the panes, brushing branches against the glass.

CHAPTER 47

Nick stared from the pavement at the derelict house. It was the address that they'd been given for Wendy Palmer, the registered owner of the silver VW Golf. 'Looks like a bloody war zone.'

The house crouched at the end of a litter-strewn cul-de-sac in Bentilee, a sketchy part of Stoke-on-Trent, half its windows boarded, the others smashed. Ripped bin bags leaked their contents across the cracked pavement. Beer cans, takeaway boxes, a child's broken scooter. Graffiti scrawled in white paint across the front door: *NO GO ZONE*.

Kennedy tucked her scarf closer to her face. It was getting cold. 'I can't believe that anyone actually lives here,' she stated, pulling a face.

'No,' Nick agreed.

Kennedy gave him a quizzical look. 'And we think Alfie might be inside?'

'It's all we've got at the moment,' Nick said in a resigned tone.

The wind picked up and bit at their faces as they walked down the uneven, weed-strewn path towards the boarded-up front door. Daylight seemed to have slipped behind a line of thick, metallic grey clouds. Dry leaves scattered across the nearby driveway in restless spirals, the sound like whispers underfoot.

Nick pulled his coat tighter, his nose wrinkling at the sharp tang of mould and old wood that leaked from the broken windowpanes. He checked his watch.

It was one p.m. An hour before the gang's deadline.

Kennedy said nothing. Her eyes were fixed on the first floor.

'Everything okay?' Nick asked under his breath.

'It's hard to tell,' she admitted. 'I thought I saw a net curtain move. But it could be the wind.'

Nick's stomach tightened. *Please let Alfie be inside.*

He glanced up to the window where there was no glass left to shield it from the wind.

Suddenly, a crow came flapping out of the house, cawing loudly and then rising above them, wings flapping low over the chimney stack, before vanishing into the gloom.

It startled them both.

They got to the end of the weed-choked path.

Nick gave the front door a solid kick. Nothing. Just the dull thud of boot against rotted wood.

There was a flimsy-looking padlock holding some of the wood in place.

'I think I've got some bolt cutters?' Kennedy suggested.

'Bollocks to that,' Nick said as he stepped back. 'Right.'

With a grunt, Nick drove his foot hard against the door's lock panel. The wood splintered, then gave way, swinging inward with a crash. A cloud of dust puffed up from the frame. The smell hit them instantly. Musty damp, decay, something darker beneath.

Something was wrong.

'Jesus.' Kennedy pulled her scarf up over her mouth. 'What the bloody hell is that?'

Nick didn't flinch as he just stepped through and took out a torch.

They both stopped. Listening for the faintest of sound or movement.

Nothing but the muffled sound of wind.

Inside, the air was thick and damp.

Their torch beams swept over peeling wallpaper, curled like old skin, and a hallway scattered with takeaway cartons, broken glass and old syringes. The floor creaked with every step. A water-stained ceiling sagged in the corner, ready to collapse.

Nick kept his voice low. 'Looks like squatters have been in here.'

'Maybe. Or someone's been using it as a trap house. Wouldn't be the first time.'

A 'trap house' was a slang term for a house or building where illegal drug activities took place, especially the selling of drugs. The word 'trap' comes from southern US street slang, where 'trapping' means dealing drugs.

They moved quietly from room to room, checking behind doors, stepping over debris.

There was no sign of Alfie or that anyone had been inside the house for months – maybe even years.

The kitchen looked like it hadn't functioned for a long time. Cupboard doors hanging off, a fridge leaking brown liquid from the base. There was more graffiti on the walls. A crude drawing of a child's face, scratched in biro, stared back at them from a cupboard door.

Then the smell intensified.

Kennedy paused at the bottom of the stairs. 'Can you smell that?'

Nick nodded. He'd smelled that stench before. It was a smell you never forgot. 'Something's dead in here.'

'It could be animal,' Kennedy said.

Nick pointed to the stairs. 'It's coming from up there.'

He led the way up the filthy wooden steps, torch trembling slightly in his grip, the beam sweeping over damp-stained walls and a line of children's stickers still stuck to the railing.

The upstairs was darker. There were two bedrooms and a bathroom which was doorless and open.

In the back bedroom, a filthy mattress lay on the floor. Black mould crept up the walls. A line of candles sat hardened and unused on the window ledge next to a bowl full of old cigarette butts.

Nick moved cautiously towards the wardrobe, its doors hanging open, and swept his torch inside. Nothing.

They went out onto the landing.

The bathroom door creaked slightly. The smell was stronger now.

Nick stepped in first with Kennedy close behind.

The small window above the toilet had been smashed, its glass glittering across the cracked tiles. Something dark was bundled beside the radiator.

He crouched and used his torch beam.

Then they saw it.

A cat.

Or what was left of one. It was half-decomposed, its collar caught around the pipe, twisted and locked, trapping it there. The poor thing had likely tried to wriggle free, panic scratched into the linoleum. It had died facing the wall.

A terrible stillness hung in the room.

Kennedy crouched and groaned. 'Bloody hell. That explains the smell.'

Nick nodded and went out onto the landing. He was frustrated.

'Alfie's not here,' he groaned. 'And there's nothing here that suggests that he has been.'

Kennedy gave Nick a dark look. 'Back to square one, Sarge.'

Nick nodded. 'Check out the back as we're here.'

'Yeah.'

They made their way downstairs again.

Outside, the back yard was more wasteland than garden. Bricks, weeds, an old, rusted BBQ.

There was no sign of recent use.

They returned to the car.

Nick looked back one last time at the house. The broken door creaked in the wind. Somewhere nearby, a dog barked once, sharp and distant.

They were still no closer to finding Alfie.

'Okay if I drive, Sarge?' Kennedy asked.

'Knock yourself out,' Nick said as he tossed her the keys.

Settling into the passenger seat, Nick's head was whirring. Where was Alfie being held? He couldn't believe that they were going to have to let Ray Clarke leave protective custody so that Alfie could be released. It was beyond frustrating.

'I'd better ring the boss and give her the good news,' Nick said sardonically.

As they drove out of the cul-de-sac, Nick grabbed his phone from his pocket and the screen lit up.

For some reason, he was drawn to watch the most recent video that British Action had sent over.

The video started. Alfie's bruised face full of fear. The vile scumbag with the hunting knife held in one gloved hand.

'We getting fucked off waiting for you, Ray. So, this is a new message for you.'

Nick searched the frame, squinting, looking for any tiny detail that would give them a clue to the location.

Nothing.

'You've got until two o'clock. That's your deadline. Two o'clock today, Ray. You tell the police, the CPS, everyone, that you're out. That you're not going to trial. That you're not giving evidence.'

Then the camera moved as the man grabbed Alfie's right hand and forced it down onto the tabletop. The man pushed Alfie's hand down hard, spreading out his fingers. Then he took the knife's blade and pushed it hard into Alfie's forefinger.

Out of the corner of his eye, Nick spotted something on the wall.

What's that?

Taking a breath, Nick paused the video. There was something white on the wall on the far left-hand corner of the screen.

Taking a screenshot, Nick then used his fingers to make the image bigger.

There was a corner of something white on the wall.

And there was something printed in black.

-ty 40.

'Stop the car,' Nick said urgently.

'What?' Kennedy looked concerned.

'It's okay,' Nick reassured her and then gestured to the image on his phone screen. 'I just need to show you this.'

Kennedy frowned as she pulled over to the side of the road. 'Okay.' They stopped.

'Tell me what you can see,' Nick said as he handed the phone.

For a few seconds, Kennedy didn't respond.

But then she saw it.

'Oh, my God. The flag,' she whispered as she looked at him. 'That's the back bedroom at Ian Nesbitt's house.'

Nick nodded as he took the phone and rang Ruth.

'Nick? Tell me you've found Alfie at that house,' Ruth said hopefully.

'No. But we know where he is,' Nick said. 'Ian Nesbitt's house. There's a part of a flag on the wall in the last video they sent us.'

'You're sure?' Ruth asked.

'Positive,' he replied. 'If we hammer it, we can be in Market Drayton in twenty minutes.'

'I'll talk to Staffordshire Police,' Ruth said. 'And I'll get armed officers to meet you there.'

'Great.' Nick hung up and looked at Kennedy. Her jaw was clenched, hands gripping the wheel.

She slammed the car into gear. 'Let's go and get him.'

The clock was ticking. There was less than an hour to go.

CHAPTER 48

Ruth took a sharp breath. Her head was whirring with thoughts of Alfie being held at Ian Nesbitt's home. Or was it going to be yet another dead end? Her boots skidded slightly on the tiled floor as she turned the corner into the hallway and nearly collided with Jane.

'Where's Rob?' Ruth asked.

'He's in the back room,' Jane said, stepping aside, her voice low. 'On a secure call to the Head of Counter Terrorism. He's updating them about Ray backing out. Not a conversation I'd want to be having.'

'No.' Ruth's stomach twisted at the thought. Then she glanced down the hallway towards the closed study door. Her eyes lingered on it, on the faint glow beneath. Was Rob really on that call or was he talking to someone else? The unease she'd tried to shake off returned in full force.

'What is it?' Jane asked. She clearly sensed Ruth's unease.

Ruth swallowed. *Trust no one.* That had been the rule since she'd found that there was a leak. Especially not when Patricia Hoskins, the CPS lawyer who'd been pushing for every strategic delay, had suddenly vanished from view on two weeks of 'personal leave'.

She looked at Jane. Really looked at her. Jane had stood by them through every moment of chaos. If Ruth couldn't trust her now, who was left?

She made the decision.

'We think we've found Alfie,' Ruth said, her voice barely audible above a whisper. 'Nick just matched the room from Alfie's video. There's a St George's flag with slogans on the wall. It's definitely Ian Nesbitt's place in Market Drayton.'

Jane froze. 'Are you sure?'

'Yes, we're certain. We've already got an ARU en route,' Ruth explained.

Behind them, there were footsteps as Sheila emerged from the kitchen. Ray followed, his coat over one arm.

Then Sheila stopped and frowned at them, her head tilted.

'What did you just say?' she asked.

Ruth stepped towards her. 'We know where Alfie is,' she said. 'We're going to get him right now.'

A moment of silence. Sheila blinked with a flicker of hope but then it was gone again.

'No,' she said. 'It's too late.'

Ray looked at her, alarmed. 'Sheila?'

'We've made our decision,' she said, louder now, looking at Ruth. 'We're done here. Ray won't testify.'

'Sheila?' Ruth said, her voice calm but firm.

'Our son is in a basement somewhere, tied to a chair, terrified,' Sheila snapped. 'And you want us to stay here? We're meant to hope that you've got it right this time or that you can rescue him. No, thank you.'

Ruth drew closer. 'We know where he is. We're this close, but if you walk out that door...'

Sheila hissed. 'He's our son.'

'Exactly,' Ruth said as her voice dropped. 'And that's why you can't go.' She turned to Ray and continued. 'Ray, you said you'd do anything to protect your family. This is the moment.'

Ray looked at Chelsie as her hands gripped the pink strap of her rucksack. She stared up at him.

'You're manipulating him,' Sheila said angrily.

'No,' Ruth said. 'I'm giving him a chance to be brave and do the right thing for once.'

Silence.

'You're certain you know where Alfie is?' Ray asked.

'Yes. Positive.'

Then Ray nodded, almost to himself. 'Then we stay.'

Sheila turned away sharply, nostrils flaring. 'Jesus, Ray. You idiot!' She walked away and out of the house.

Ruth exhaled slowly in relief. 'Thank you, Ray. We're going to get Alfie back to you safely. And then we're going to put those men away for the rest of their lives.'

CHAPTER 49

The cul-de-sac in Market Drayton was silent. Nick squinted through the windscreen of the unmarked police car as the decrepit two-storey house came into view. Ivy clawed up cracked brickwork, and the windows were stained with a nicotine yellow hue.

Kennedy pulled the car to a gentle stop, twenty metres from the house, trying to keep it nestled behind a thick hedgerow. The Armed Response Vehicle behind them did the same, its tinted windows hiding the six AROs inside.

Kennedy shifted in her seat, tension in her face, holding the steering wheel tight.

Nick hesitated as he glanced up at the house. It was still. If someone had spotted their arrival, they weren't showing it. Or maybe it was empty.

Nick glanced at the time on his phone. One fifty-six p.m.

'Just in time,' Nick said under his breath as he showed her.

Kennedy gave him a dark look. 'Unless they've moved him.'

The memory of Alfie's face in the hostage video, bruised, scared, but alive, flickered across his mind. They were going in there to get him back from those sick bastards. Nick could feel the adrenaline coursing through his veins.

They got out slowly and headed to the back of the unmarked Astra.

Kennedy opened the boot and handed him the heavy Kevlar vest.

'Here you go, Sarge.'

'Thanks,' he said.

Then she blew out her cheeks. He could see she was nervous.

'Don't worry,' Nick said, trying to reassure her. 'We'll let the Shots do their thing.'

Nick looked down the road and gave the signal.

The six AROs emerged from their vehicle like shadows. Silent, masked, disciplined.

They fanned out behind him and Kennedy as they approached the crumbling front garden in silence.

Kennedy muttered, her eyes flicking over the windows. 'No lights. No movement. Maybe they really have cleared out.'

Nick pulled a face. 'Christ, I really hope not.' He then clicked his radio and said in a virtual whisper, 'Gold Command, this is three-six. We're at target location. Suspects inside will be armed and dangerous. We have a teenage male hostage inside, so proceed with caution, over.'

'Received, three-six,' came the crackling response. 'No engagement unless fired upon. Gold Command out.'

Nick tucked the radio away. 'Let's see if we can see inside before they go charging in.'

Nick watched as two AROs moved swiftly down the side of the house towards the back. They didn't want Alfie being taken out through the back garden and disappearing.

They stepped over the broken gate and into the overgrown garden. Empty beer cans littered the path.

Nick went to a downstairs window, cupped his hands and looked inside. All he could see was the empty living room. It was in darkness.

It wasn't a good sign.

He glanced at Kennedy and then at the lead ARO and shook his head.

Nothing.

Wind stirred the dead leaves around their feet. A broken gutter clanged gently above.

Crouching down, Nick then very slowly pushed open the letterbox and listened intently. His heart was pounding against his chest.

From within, the scrape of movement.

What was that?

A whispered voice, too quiet to hear properly. Then silence.

Turning his head, Nick squinted to look inside.

His eyes focused on someone standing at the bottom of the stairs.

Someone was standing there, dressed in military boots and combat fatigues. They were still and not moving.

Shit. Have they spotted the letterbox opening? Am I about to get shot?

He held his breath, not daring to move the metallic letterbox in case it squeaked and gave him away.

The boots turned and walked very carefully and very slowly up the stairs. The deliberately cautious movement could mean only one thing.
They know we're here.
Taking a breath to steady himself, Nick lowered the letterbox inch by inch until it was closed.
Before Nick could tell Kennedy and the ARO what he'd seen, Kennedy's gaze was taken up to the first floor.
'Sarge...' she whispered with an urgent nod up to the first floor.
He held up a hand to signal that they needed to be completely silent. Glancing up, Nick then focused on the window above them.
Nothing.
He gave Kennedy a quizzical look.
Then it came. A flicker of movement at an upstairs window. A bearded man's face – he was holding something.
Is that a gun?
The man looked down at them.
Shit!
Silence.
Suddenly the man threw the window open and pointed a semi-automatic weapon at them, locking it into this shoulder.
'Gun!' Kennedy hissed.
'GET DOWN!' Nick yelled.
CRACK! CRACK! CRACK!
The air exploded with the sound of automatic gunfire.
Nick grabbed Kennedy's shoulder and dragged her to the ground as an ARO returned fire.
Bullets shattered the upper window and slammed into the crumbling brick beside them.
Nick and Kennedy scrambled to the front wall of the house for cover.
'Hold your fire!' Nick bellowed. 'Our hostage might be up there.'
The AROs quickly took cover behind hedges and a garden wall, weapons trained on the windows but fingers off triggers.
'This is not good,' Kennedy gasped, her breathing heavy.
CRACK!
Another shot. This one lower and much closer.
The stone from the garden path exploded about two feet from where Nick and Kennedy crouched. Shrapnel flying everywhere.

Nick flinched, his eyes wide. How the hell were they going to get out of this? They were pinned down.

'We're trapped,' Kennedy said, pressing her back against the wall.

Nick's mind raced. 'We were set up. They knew we were coming. How the hell are we going to get Alfie out of there now?'

Kennedy shook her head.

Another bullet smashed into the path nearby throwing stone and earth into the air.

'Bloody hell!' Kennedy hissed as she flinched again. She looked at Nick. 'Options?'

He shook his head. 'We can't return fire. Not if Alfie is inside.'

'We don't actually know that he is in there,' Kennedy said.

Another bullet pinged off the ground in front of them.

'He has to be in there. And they know we can't shoot back if he is,' Nick growled in frustration. Then he had a thought. 'Wait there.'

Kennedy gave him a withering look. 'Where the hell are you going?'

Crouched low, Nick sprinted across the front of the house and back to the front door. Pushing open the letter box, he looked inside again.

Moving up the stairs were two pairs of legs. One dressed in boots and fatigues. The other in trackies and trainers.

Alfie.

Alfie was definitely inside.

They needed a plan B for his rescue.

Nick grabbed his radio. 'All units, this is three-six. You are authorised to withdraw to safety. Repeat, you are authorised to withdraw to safety.'

Nick scurried back to Kennedy. 'Alfie's definitely in there. Come on. We're pulling back.'

Kennedy followed him as they bolted, crouching low, running for their lives.

Behind them, the AROs slowly retreated, eyes and guns still locked on the house.

CRACK!

A shot rang out.

Kennedy dropped like a stone to the pavement behind Nick.

'Jesus,' Nick gasped as he turned and ran back to her.

CRACK.

Another shot ran out and Nick ducked.

A few seconds later, two AROs hurried over.

Grabbing the top of Kennedy's Kevlar vest, they dragged her down the pavement and behind the vehicles for cover.

Nick crouched down and looked.

'Jade? Jade?' Nick said frantically as he searched her for a bullet wound.

She didn't respond.

CHAPTER 50

Ruth took a long, anxious drag of her cigarette as she stood looking over Bala Lake. But she couldn't concentrate on the view. Five minutes earlier, she'd had an emergency report of gunfire from the operation at Ian Nesbitt's house in Market Drayton. Details were sketchy. She'd been unable to contact Nick, Kennedy or the Armed Response Unit. It made her sick with worry. Were her officers okay and safe? Had Alfie been rescued?

Blowing out smoke, she squinted down at the haze hanging over the lake. The watery surface was so still.

She tried Nick again. Straight to voicemail. A tightness gripped her chest.

Come on, Nick!

Somewhere in the trees behind her, a curlew called. A wavering, sorrowful sound that sent a ripple down her spine. Everything was too quiet.

She flicked ash from the end of her cigarette. She should have heard something by now. A message. A call. Anything.

Jane appeared on the stone steps of the safe house.

'Any news yet?' Jane asked.

Ruth shook her head. 'Nothing. What about your end?'

Jane shrugged. 'Nothing yet. The BBC are now running it as a breaking news story.'

'I'll let you know as soon as I hear anything,' Ruth reassured her, but she was unnerved.

Jane went back inside.

Ruth lit another cigarette with the dying one. Her eyes stung from the smoke. She wasn't sure how much longer she could stand here waiting. It was torture.

Then her phone rang. It was Nick.

'Boss,' Nick gasped in a frantic voice.

'What's going on?' Ruth asked anxiously.

'Listen, Jade's been shot. She's okay. Her vest took most of the force but the bullet's in her shoulder. They're taking her to the Princess Royal in Telford,' Nick explained in a calm tone.

'Jesus,' Ruth gasped. 'But she's okay?' She wanted reassuring.

'Yes. It's painful but she's going to be okay.'

'Alfie?' Ruth asked, her heart now pounding as she took all this in.

'He's still in there. I saw him,' Nick said. 'We've had to retreat and regroup. They were waiting for us and opened fire. They knew we were coming, boss.'

'What?' Ruth said as her mind ticked away. 'But you're certain that Alfie is inside?'

'I saw him,' Nick replied.

Ruth took a moment. Then her heart sank. 'The only person that knew you were going to Ian Nesbitt's address was Jane Robinson.'

'Right,' Nick said. 'That's not good.'

'No. But I'll deal with that here,' Ruth said. 'You're on the ground there. What's our next move?'

'The AROs think we'll have to send in the Specialist Tactical Firearms Unit,' Nick explained. 'Unless you want us to bring in a hostage negotiator?'

'No,' Ruth said, trying to think through every scenario. 'I don't want them cutting off Alfie's fingers while we try to negotiate. I'm going to need to talk to the chief constable but expect a TFU to be with you in the next hour.'

'Yes, boss,' Nick said. 'I'll keep you posted.'

'And Nick?'

'Boss?'

'Be safe, please,' Ruth sighed.

'Will do.'

Ruth slipped her phone back into her coat pocket. The wind had shifted again, colder now.

She heard the door creak behind her. Jane moved out onto the steps once more, arms folded tight against the chill.

'Still nothing?' Jane asked, a little too casual.

'No,' Ruth said flatly. 'Still nothing.'

She could feel Jane's eyes on her, trying to read her face. But Ruth kept her expression blank. Inside, though, her stomach twisted with what she now suspected.

Jane lingered for a moment longer, then went back inside. The door shut softly behind her.

Ruth stared out at the lake again, her cigarette burning down between her fingers.

She dropped the butt, ground it into the gravel with her heel, and pulled out her phone once more. Her thumb hovered for just a second before she found the number and pressed CALL.

It rang twice.

'Chief constable's office?' said a female voice when the line picked up.

'Is he in? This is an emergency,' Ruth explained. 'It's DI Ruth Hunter, SIO on the Ashwin Choudary murder investigation.'

'I'll put you through.'

'Ruth.'

'Sir.'

'What is it?' he asked.

'I need your authorisation to deploy a Specialist Tactical Firearms Unit to an address in Market Drayton, sir. I'm sure you're already aware but we now have a hostage situation. The son of our key witness,' Ruth said.

'Yes. I'm being kept updated with the developments.' There was a pause on the other end. 'I assume that the TFU is a last resort?'

'Yes, sir. But the kidnappers have given us and our witness an ultimatum. They start harming the hostage after two p.m. We're running out of time,' Ruth explained.

'Then consider it done.'

'Thank you,' Ruth said relieved.

She ended the call and stood for a moment, the wind catching her coat and pushing her hair into her face.

Then she looked at her phone, found a number and dialled it.

The phone rang.

'Hello, Counter Corruption Unit,' said a male voice.

'This is Detective Inspector Ruth Hunter, North Wales Police,' Ruth said. 'I need to flag up my suspicions about a fellow officer, Detective Constable Jane Robinson.'

'Could you hold please and I'll transfer you,' the voice said.
The lake below was beginning to ripple now, the stillness broken. Something had shifted.

CHAPTER 51

Nick crouched behind the cordon tape at the edge of the cul-de-sac in Market Drayton. Uniformed officers in high-vis jackets were ushering the last stragglers – curious neighbours, anxious dog walkers – out of harm's way. Patrol cars and ambulances sat with blue lights strobing but no sirens, only the low murmur of radios and the patter of persistent drizzle.

The rain speckled the hood of his jacket, glistening on his eyelashes. Evening had dropped like a shroud, the air thick with the kind of tension Nick had come to associate with an armed incident. The moment before detonation.

He rubbed a drying smear of blood from the heel of his palm. It was Kennedy's. When he'd dragged her behind cover after the sniper round hit, he hadn't registered it. She was alive and stable in the ICU at Telford. But Nick could still hear the thud of her body hitting the pavement, the way her arm had jerked in a grotesque arc. That image would stay with him.

He'd already made a call to the hospital. Kennedy was now conscious and lucid which was a relief. She'd even asked him about Alfie and asked to be kept informed of any developments.

From somewhere behind the grey rooftops came the growing thrum of rotor blades. A black Eurocopter Dauphin punched through the misted sky. It dropped low, rattling windows, knocking over a wheelie bin with the downward force of its rotors, and then settled into the clearing just beyond the estate with a mechanical grace that belied its bulk.

Then came the Tactical Firearms Unit.

Eight officers in matt-black body armour, faces masked, visors down, Heckler & Koch semi-automatics held low. There was no talking, just cold efficiency.

The lead officer approached. He flicked his visor up to reveal calm, unreadable eyes, a dark beard and a deep scar across his right eyebrow.

'DS Evans?' His accent was Scottish but Nick couldn't place it exactly.

Nick nodded. 'Yeah. That's me.'

The helicopter rotors ticked down behind them with a descending whine.

'What have we got in there?' the officer asked in a terse and direct tone.

'Two confirmed suspects. They're armed but I think there are probably more. One had a semi-automatic which I spotted through an upstairs window.' Nick pointed to the house. 'They've got a hostage. A fifteen-year-old boy, Alfie Clarke. Grey trackies and white Nike trainers.' Nick glanced at the time on his phone. It was three thirty-six p.m. 'They gave us a deadline of two p.m., so I'm worried that they're going to harm Alfie.'

The officer tilted his head, absorbing what Nick had told him. 'Okay. Time we got on with this then. I'll give you a signal when the house is clear and the hostage is safe.'

'Thank you,' Nick said with a grateful nod.

And with that, the officer turned back to his team and made a series of rapid hand signals. Like clockwork, they started to move. Slinking down both flanks of the street, disappearing into shadows and angles, in well-rehearsed manoeuvres.

Nick swallowed nervously. He wouldn't be going in with them. That wasn't his role. But there was a part of him that would have loved to have breached that door, to be the one to pull Alfie out of the darkness. And if he had to put a round into that scumbag Ian Nesbitt, then so be it.

The wind changed direction and then seemed to stop in its tracks. Silence.

Then the sudden, acrid sting caught the back of Nick's throat. The CS gas had been deployed.

Nick took a breath. The calm before the storm.

Seconds later, a loud *CRASH*. Maybe a rear or side door being smashed open.

Here we go, he thought, almost holding his breath with worry.

A flash-bang erupted with a white-hot *POP* that lit the front windows of the house like a thunderclap.

Then the second assault team surged forward, battering ram up, shattering the front door inwards.

The sound of chaos.

Muffled shouting. Barked commands.

'ARMED POLICE! SHOW YOURSELVES!'

The unmistakeable *CLATTER* of automatic gunfire. Short, controlled bursts. Then another loud bang.

And then... a strained silence.

Nick stood, blowing out his cheeks, heart hammering. The adrenaline zipped through his blood. No one moved. The house stood dark, CS smoke curling out from the shattered doorway.

He took a step forward, then another, weaving between the parked cars. No word from the TFU yet but that wasn't unusual. They secured the scene first, then communicated that it was safe.

Nick continued moving, passing the smashed gatepost, boots crunching over splintered brick and broken glass. Then something caught his eye.

From the side of the house, a shadow detached itself.

A figure appeared.

A face that he recognised.

Darren Nesbitt.

Nick recognised him instantly. Blond crew cut, lean frame, the twisted grin of someone who believed he was going to escape.

Nesbitt started to sprint across the garden, a Glock 17 in his hand.

'STOP! POLICE!' Nick shouted. 'Armed suspect. East side!'

He wasn't going to wait for backup.

Nick took off after him, vaulted the low garden wall, landing hard, his ankle jarring.

Nesbitt darted into a back alley, cutting between sheds and walls.

Nick followed, breath burning in his throat from the CS gas.

They scrambled through a narrow passageway, mud slick beneath their feet. Nick hurdled a fallen wheelie bin.

Nesbitt was fast. A fence splintered as he forced his way over, and Nick used the sound to close in.

They entered a string of back gardens, each separated by sagging fences, hedgerows, compost heaps.

A cat screeched and bolted for cover.

Nick caught a glimpse of Nesbitt's profile as he turned and fired.

CRACK.

The round split the air beside Nick's head.

Jesus Christ! That was close.

He dived behind a rusting swing set, mud caking his knees, heart pounding in his ears.

Another shot cracked off a paving slab near his foot.

He popped up, caught sight of Nesbitt just as he ducked into another garden.

Nick surged after him, leaped over a hedge and landed hard, his ankle twinging again but he kept going.

This ends now, you bastard!

Nesbitt was slowing, breathing ragged, weaving through garden furniture.

Nick closed the gap. Ten yards maybe.

Nesbitt slowed again and went to take another shot.

Nick lunged and brought him down with a full-body rugby tackle that drove the air from both of them.

They hit the grass hard, fists flying.

Nesbitt clawed at Nick's face, his boot catching Nick's ribs.

Nick drove an elbow into Nesbitt's side. The handgun skittered across the lawn.

They scrambled, tangled, fists connecting with sickening thuds.

Nick's nose exploded in pain as a punch landed square. Blood flowed down his face.

Nesbitt twisted free, gasping, and crawled towards the weapon.

'No you don't...' Nick tried to grab his leg but missed.

Nesbitt's fingers wrapped around the grip. He rolled over, arm raised, closing one eye to take aim.

Nick froze.

Everything slowed. The rain. His heartbeat.

The look on Nesbitt's face. Their eyes met.

There was no doubt. Nesbitt was going to kill him.

Then...

CRACK!

A shot rang out.

Nick winced, closing his eyes. Waiting for the hot searing pain of a gunshot in his chest or abdomen.

But nothing.

He opened his eyes.

Nesbitt jerked, the pistol dropped from his hand. His chest pierced by a single bullet. He slumped, eyes wide, lifeless.

Behind them, the TFU lead officer appeared out of the shadows, lowered his weapon, and stepped through a broken fence.

'Clear!' he called over his shoulder. 'Suspect down. Officer safe.'

Nick remained crouched, his breathing hard. Blood dripped from his chin as he turned to the officer.

'Thanks,' Nick gasped.

'No problem,' the officer said in his deep Scottish brogue.

'Alfie?' Nick asked as he gasped for breath.

The officer nodded. 'Safe. Shaken and very scared. But safe. We got him out just after the breach. He's with the paramedics now.'

'Thank God.' Nick let out a long, unsteady breath. His arms were shaking. The garden spun slightly before he caught himself.

The air was filled with noise. Sirens of approaching emergency vehicles. More officers, more medics, the inevitable crime scene teams.

He glanced down at Nesbitt's body. Another wasted life. Another angry man led into hatred by poisonous politics and online forums.

Nick stood up slowly.

Around him, the estate was still. People peered from windows, some filming. The rain kept falling, but it no longer mattered.

Alfie was safe.

Kennedy was alive.

And Darren Nesbitt would never hurt anyone again.

CHAPTER 52

5 HOURS LATER

The flames in the fire pit snapped softly in the growing dusk. Smoke drifted upwards in languid curls, catching the light before disappearing into the night air. Ruth stood just beyond the circle of warmth, arms folded, watching the Clarke family gathered close around the embers. There were no words between them, just quiet comfort.

Alfie was nestled between his mother and sister, wrapped in a heavy blanket, his small shoulders rising and falling in slow rhythm. Clarke sat behind them, one hand resting on Chelsie's back, his face tipped towards the glow of the fire.

Ruth let the moment settle and didn't intrude.

Behind her, the front door clicked open.

Jane stepped out, hugging her jacket tighter against the cold. Her boots made no sound on the grass as she walked to Ruth's side. She paused there, just on the edge of the firelight, her gaze fixed on the family.

'They look... okay,' Jane said finally, her voice low as she searched for the right word. 'But Alfie, I mean. He—'

Ruth cut in, quiet but firm. 'They just need time. A lot of time.'

Jane gave a small nod, maybe sensing Ruth's underlying antagonism. They stood in silence for a moment, the air between them brittle.

'You think Ray will go through with it?' Jane asked. 'All the way to the trial?'

Ruth turned to her now. Really looked at her. Jane's eyes were dull, rimmed with the fatigue of too many days without proper rest. Or maybe it was the guilt.

Was she really leaking information to British Action? If she was, why? Money? Intimidation? Blackmail?

'I think he will. But it only works if we're completely airtight,' Ruth said in a tone that implied subtext. 'One crack, one slip, and their defence team will drive a truck through our case.'

Jane's brow tightened. 'What are you getting at?'

Ruth didn't answer. The words hovered unsaid, heavy and dangerous. She would leave it.

From the road beyond the hedgerow came headlights and the low crunch of tyres on gravel.

Ruth straightened.

The faint hum of engines followed. An unmarked black BMW, headlights dimmed, rolled to a stop by the front gate. Ruth didn't flinch. She'd been expecting them.

Instead, she turned and walked towards the gate control panel.

'You know who that is?' Jane called softly behind her.

'Yes,' Ruth replied, giving nothing away.

A pause.

'You going to tell me?' she asked with a quizzical frown.

But Ruth didn't answer. She was already keying in the code.

The gate opened slowly with a mechanical sigh.

The car parked up and two officers stepped out. They were dressed in smart clothes, their manner businesslike.

The lead officer – forties, close-cropped hair, quick eyes – raised an eyebrow. 'DI Ruth Hunter?'

Ruth's pulse had quickened. This was going to be uncomfortable but it had to be done. 'Yes.'

The officer's eyes then glanced over at Jane.

'DC Jane Robinson?' he asked in a flat voice.

Jane narrowed her eyes, confused. 'Yes?'

He took a step towards her. 'I'm DCI Phillips from the Counter Corruption Unit. I'm placing you under arrest on the suspicion of colluding with a proscribed terrorist organisation. I have a warrant here to take you in for questioning.'

The stillness in the garden fractured.

The blood drained from Jane's face as she took a step back. 'You can't be serious.'

Phillips's tone didn't waver. 'I'm going to need you to come with us right now. And I suggest that you contact your Police Federation rep on the way.'

From the side of the house, Rob appeared, moving fast. His face was tight with disbelief.

'Jane? What the hell is this?' he asked loudly.

She didn't answer for a second. Then she shook her head. 'I honestly have no idea. It's a big mistake.'

Rob looked at Ruth. 'You know anything about this?'

Ruth held his gaze but said nothing.

Jane turned to her slowly, her voice barely audible. 'Ruth?'

Ruth just looked at her.

Phillips stepped forward. 'I need you to get in the car.'

She nodded reluctantly. Her steps were slow, deliberate, as she allowed herself to be led away. No cuffs.

The Clarke family didn't move. Behind them, the fire still flickered. Alfie stared into the flames, Chelsie's head resting against Sheila's shoulder. Ray hadn't taken his eyes off his son.

It was as if they were in another world entirely.

Rob watched the officers walk over to the car with Jane in their midst. Then he turned back to Ruth, his face a mix of fury and pain.

'How can you think she's the leak? You're way off here,' he said angrily.

Ruth didn't respond.

'This is bullshit.' Rob stepped back, shaking his head, and disappeared into the house.

The fire popped suddenly, sending a brief spray of sparks into the night.

Ruth turned away from them and stared at the darkened lane beyond the gate, where red taillights had vanished into the distance.

She didn't feel victory.

And far off, in the trees, a fox shrieked. The sound was sharp, startled, and strange.

The wind shifted.

The fire crackled in a low tone.

And Ruth knew this wasn't the end. Not yet.

CHAPTER 53

The incident room at Llancastell nick was thick with the stale smell of coffee and tension. The early morning sunlight filtered weakly through dusty blinds, casting narrow bands of light across the whiteboards plastered with crime scene photos, maps of Bangor, the coastline and Post-it notes.

Ruth stood at the front of the room, her back to the board. Then she perched on the edge of a table. She could still feel the tension in her neck and shoulders. She took a breath, let it sit for a moment, and then began. 'Right. Before anything else, I want to thank you all. What we pulled off last night, tracking down and getting Alfie out alive, was outstanding work. I know that the TFU will get all the plaudits.'

'They always do,' Nick said. 'But they saved my life last night so I'm not going to complain.'

A few nods. Garrow scratched his beard and looked thoughtful.

'A quick update,' Ruth continued. 'Jade is still at the Royal Princess but she's being moved over to Llancastell University Hospital this morning. As most of you know, Jade took a round to the shoulder, clean entry and exit, no major nerve damage. She's already complaining about the food and trying to get her laptop brought in. So, I think we can safely say she's on the mend.'

A ripple of tired laughter broke across the room, the kind that came from relief rather than humour.

'And Alfie...' Ruth hesitated, her voice catching in her chest for a fraction of a second. 'He's safe. The trauma response team has him under observation. Social Services brought in a crisis carer. He hasn't said much yet, but that's to be expected.' Ruth exhaled, her gaze hardening slightly. 'Darren Nesbitt was shot and killed by a TFU officer during the operation. Bodycam footage confirms he raised a weapon to shoot Nick. The officer had no choice. That said, a full IOPC inquiry is underway. We will co-operate fully so I want no crossed wires, no omitted statements. Do we understand?'

A collective nod. Nick tapped a pen against his notepad, thoughtful. Garrow glanced at him, then spoke up. 'Any word on Ian Nesbitt?'

'Gone,' Ruth said, her jaw tightening. 'His burner phone went offline an hour before we breached the property. No sightings, no flagged travel documents. We've got alerts across every port, train station, but so far, nothing. And now,' she went on, stepping back to the board, 'Counter Terrorism will be taking a more hands-on role. The CPS is preparing to prosecute British Action's leadership over the murder of Ashwin Choudary, and the CTD need our full support.'

The map beside her had been annotated overnight. Lines drawn from Bangor to Stoke, then outward towards Cardiff and London.

'But we will need to expect some friction,' she said warily. 'The arrest of DC Jane Robinson hit Counter Terrorism hard. They're not exactly extending warm invitations to us. But that doesn't change what we have to do. This is about justice for Ashwin and his family. We keep our focus. We gather everything. Emails, surveillance logs, financial trails, phone data. If someone so much as donated a tenner to British Action's slush fund, I want it documented.' She turned back to them. 'Garrow, you've spoken to the CPS?'

He nodded. 'I spoke to a Felicity Barnes first thing. She clarified something about Patricia Hoskins's leave. Apparently, her father died. He had a sudden cardiac arrest. That's why she took two weeks off with no notice.'

Ruth's features softened. She felt a pang of guilt that she'd had Hoskins in her crosshairs as the source of the leak. 'Let's send a condolence card. And the CCTV from the retail park in Stoke. The woman handing Darren the Glock, is there any update?'

Nick leaned forward, elbows on the table. 'Digital Forensics are still analysing and cleaning up the footage. We've requested enhancement. They're going to try facial recognition, gait analysis, height profile. The image is grainy, but the outline...' He didn't finish the sentence.

'Is it Robinson?' Garrow asked, the question landing like a stone.

Ruth hesitated. 'I hope to God it's not,' she said, barely above a whisper.

She turned to the board and uncapped a red marker. Across the top right, someone had written one word in capital letters.

WOLF?

Nick's voice was quiet but direct. 'Could she be Wolf?'

Ruth's heart sank a little. 'It's possible. She had access to the ops schedules, to arrest warrants, security codes. She knew where we'd be. She could have tipped them off more than once, and we wouldn't have known it.'

Garrow rubbed a hand over his face. 'Jesus. The whole time she was with you and the Clarke family?'

'She fooled all of us,' Ruth said. 'Including me.'

The silence in the room deepened.

Only the faint hum of traffic on the road outside.

Ruth took a long sip of lukewarm coffee. 'Right, thank you, everyone. We still have lots of work to be getting on with.'

The room stayed still for a moment, then slowly began to stir. Chairs scraped. Notepads closed. The team began filtering off one by one.

Only Ruth remained at the board, her eyes fixed on the name *WOLF*, now underlined twice in red.

CHAPTER 54

72 HOURS LATER

The low chime of Bangor Cathedral's bell carried on the crisp air, solemn and hollow, as though it too grieved for the man they were here to remember. Ruth stood at the edge of the churchyard, shoulder to shoulder with Nick, both of them silent for a long while. The sun angled low in the autumn sky, casting a warm gold glow across the slate roofs and ancient sandstone walls of the cathedral.

Bangor Cathedral, a modest yet dignified structure nestled into the hillside above the Menai Strait. Founded in the sixth century by Saint Deiniol and rebuilt in the twelfth century, its Romanesque arches and weathered tower bore the weight of time with quiet grace. Today, its arched doors stood open, light pooling from within, illuminating the dark interior where mourners filtered through like shadows.

Politicians in dark suits and women in long coats and hats stood in quiet clusters around the forecourt, their voices low, the weight of public duty hanging over their bowed heads. Ashwin Choudary had been a divisive figure in Westminster, but no one could deny the senselessness of his murder. Executed in broad daylight by Darren Nesbitt, British Action's foot soldier. A monster bred by ideology.

Nick's phone buzzed, breaking the spell. He frowned, pulled it from his pocket, and stepped away without a word.

Ruth didn't watch him go. Her eyes drifted across the gathered mourners. She recognised several MPs – some local, others from the capital – flanked by aides and private security. There were community leaders too, one or two priests, and even a rabbi and imam standing side by side in quiet conversation. It felt like a gesture of unity in the face of something so terrible and tragic.

She crossed her arms tightly, fingers curling under the sleeves of her coat. The investigation had taken everything out of her. She hadn't slept for more than a few hours at a stretch in weeks. But today, she allowed herself a glimmer of satisfaction. The net was tightening around British Action. Ray Clarke's testimony had exposed the upper echelons. The planning meetings, the coded language, the funding trails. There would be trials and hopefully decades in prison for the leadership. It wouldn't bring Ashwin back, but it would send a message.

She turned as Nick came back towards her, his gait slower, his brow drawn tight. Something in his expression chilled her before he'd even opened his mouth.

'What is it?' she asked.

He hesitated. 'That was Sophie Hall from the Counter Corruption Unit. They've closed the file on Jane Robinson.'

Ruth blinked. 'What do you mean, "closed"?'

'They've dropped all charges. No evidence of collusion. Nothing. They've gone through every call, every message, every email. Personal and professional. Timeline analysis, metadata, the lot.'

Ruth shook her head slowly, the certainty she'd clung to slipping away. 'That doesn't make sense. She was the only one that had that access. She was in the right places at the right times. She knew every move that we were making.'

'I know.' Nick's voice was flat. 'But it can't be her.'

For a moment, Ruth stood rooted, the sounds of the memorial fading behind the thunder of her thoughts. She hated being wrong. But if not Jane, then who? Who had betrayed them?

She looked at Nick. They were thinking the same thing.

'Rob?' she said.

'Has to be,' Nick agreed.

Before they could continue, Garrow called.

'Jim?' Ruth said, answering her phone.

'Boss,' Garrow said.

'Everything all right?'

'We've got a bit of bombshell here,' Garrow said. 'I've sent you a video to look at CCTV from the Stoke retail park. The one from the night before the shooting. It's been cleaned up by Digital Forensics,' he explained. 'Facial recognition picked up the woman who gave Nesbitt the gun.'

Her heart ticked faster as she grabbed her phone and searched for the video. She was confused. 'Was it Jane?'

'No, boss,' Garrow said in a dark tone.

Ruth leaned close to watch the video on her phone as Nick peered over to watch.

The image was grainy but clear enough. A woman in a dark hoodie, standing beneath the cold glow of a streetlight beside a closed sofa shop. Her face turned slightly towards the camera. Familiar. Too familiar.

Ruth's breath caught. 'That's… that's Sheila Clarke.'

'Jesus!' Nick said.

Ruth stepped back as if the truth was too much. She looked away, jaw tightening, and then back at the image. 'No. That doesn't make sense. Why is she handing Darren Nesbitt the gun?'

Nick looked at her, thinking. 'Sheila knew every move we were making.'

Ruth tried to piece it together. Nick was right. Sheila knew the location of the safe house, the gate code, the raid on Bowie's scrapyard and the operation to rescue Alfie from Ian Nesbitt's home.

'Why would she want her own son taken hostage?' Ruth said thinking out loud.

'No idea.' Nick shifted beside her. 'You think Ray knew?'

'No. I don't know… Thank you, Jim. That is a bombshell,' Ruth admitted.

'Yes, boss,' Garrow said.

Ruth's pulse quickened. 'Jim, I need you to ring the safe house now. Tell DS Felix Butler that Sheila Clarke isn't to leave on any account. If she tries to leave, tell him to arrest her. Tell him that Nick and I are on our way.'

Ruth ended the call, her head spinning with what she'd seen in the video.

Inside the cathedral, the choir began to sing. A low, aching lament in Welsh that rose into the vaulted nave.

'Come on, we need to go,' Ruth said with a sense of urgency as they hurried towards the car.

'If Sheila Clarke was the one who armed Nesbitt, she's not just an accessory. She's central to everything,' Nick said as they broke into a jog. 'Conspiracy, supply of the firearm, and possibly the mastermind behind the assassination.'

The sun slipped behind a cloud, dimming the graveyard to greys and browns.

As they arrived at the car, Ruth tossed Nick the car keys. 'You drive, I'll smoke.'

CHAPTER 55

The hills rolled out before them like burnished copper, bracken already tinged with rust as mist crawled across the valley floor. The unmarked police Astra climbed steadily along the winding A4212 through Snowdonia, the road snaking between moss-dark rock and flaming groves of beech and rowan. The silence in the car had stretched on too long.

Ruth took a final drag of her cigarette, watching the smoke curl out of the open window into the crisp autumn air. She flicked the butt out, watching it tumble onto the verge.

'I keep seeing her face,' she said finally. 'In that bloody fleece. Crying over Alfie, saying how scared she was. When all the time...'

Nick glanced sideways, one hand on the wheel. 'All the time she was feeding us a load of crap.'

Ruth nodded, her jaw tight. 'Sheila Clarke. Jesus. She was hiding in plain sight. I keep going over it. They've only been married a couple of years.'

Nick snorted softly. 'Convenient timing, don't you think?'

Ruth's phone buzzed in her jacket pocket. She fished it out and answered without preamble. 'Garrow. What have you got?'

The line crackled for a second before his voice came through. 'You're not going to like this, boss.'

'Go on,' she said warily. She'd asked him to run Sheila Clarke through the PNC and HOLMES databases. She then tapped the button so that her phone was on speaker and Nick could hear what Garrow was about to tell her.

'Sheila Clarke's maiden name's Sheila Martin. She was convicted of attempted murder in 2000. A female Asian victim in Derby. She spent eight years in Holloway.'

Jesus!

Ruth felt her stomach tighten. 'Anything else?'

'In 2010 she was arrested for distributing racially inflammatory material at Aston University. Nazi propaganda. In 2013, she was caught with a machete in a lock-up in Birmingham. Along with posters, leaflets and other Nazi paraphernalia.'

Nick let out a low whistle.

Ruth shook her head. 'You're telling me that the woman I've been drinking tea with is a convicted psychotic racist extremist?'

'Looks that way. And, boss, one more thing. Counter Terrorism flagged her in 2018 as being the person they'd codenamed "Wolf". Nothing came of it.'

'For God's sake!' Ruth groaned. 'How the hell did we miss all this? Okay, thanks, Jim.'

Ruth ended the call and let the silence sit heavy between her and Nick.

She shook her head. 'Are we saying that Sheila Clarke is this "Wolf"?'

'It's a strong possibility. She fits the profile. Clean record for over a decade. She keeps a low profile,' Nick said. 'Then she marries a man like Ray Clarke. He's a foot soldier and not the sharpest tool in the box. It's the perfect cover.'

'She planned all this,' Ruth said quietly. 'She married Ray so she could stay close to British Action. Use the marriage as cover. She leaked intel about the safe house. Then she helped them snatch Alfie. And all the time, she played the doting stepmum.'

Nick sighed, 'Wow. It was all a bloody act.'

Ruth's voice was brittle. 'She's been sitting under our noses. The whole time. And she handed the gun to Nesbitt herself. To kill Choudary. What an absolute shitshow this has been from the beginning.'

Neither of them spoke for a long moment.

Then Nick murmured, 'She's good. I'll give her that. A wolf in sheep's clothing.'

But Ruth didn't want to entertain that thought.

'Is that supposed to be funny?' Ruth sighed.

'No, boss.'

They descended now towards Bala, the silver sweep of the lake emerging between the folds of the hills. The sky above was bruised with low cloud, but the light still picked out the tops of the trees and the long stone wall lining the road like an old scar.

As they pulled up through the gates of the safe house, Ruth caught sight of her.

Sheila sat outside on a wooden bench, blanket drawn around her shoulders, a chipped mug cradled in both hands. She stared out over the lake as if she didn't have a care in the world. A picture of serenity.

Ruth got out slowly, her boots crunching on the gravel. Nick followed, leaving the engine running.

'Sheila Clarke,' Ruth called, unable to hide her anger.

Sheila turned, her expression unreadable.

'I'm arresting you for conspiracy to commit racially motivated murder, kidnapping, and assisting an offender.'

Sheila didn't move. She blinked once, then let out a soft breath. Slowly, she stood and placed the mug on the bench.

There was no protest. No questions. Just a faint, knowing smile that curled at the corner of her mouth.

Ruth stepped forward and clicked the cuffs on. 'Anything you say may be used in evidence.'

Sheila gave a small nod. 'Of course.'

As they led her to the car, she glanced up at the hills.

'Beautiful country,' she murmured. 'Wasted on most people.'

Ruth felt a chill trace her spine despite the still air.

They put Sheila into the back seat. Ruth closed the door and looked across at Nick. He gave her a serious but satisfied look.

As they drove off, the lake in front of them rippled in the breeze.

CHAPTER 56

Ruth hovered by the edge of the hospital bed, arms folded, eyes narrowing with suspicion. 'Sure you're not just milking all this for sympathy, Jade?' she teased her, a grin threatening the corners of her mouth.

Kennedy raised her good arm and gave a mock scowl. The other was strapped up, the white hospital gown making her look more fragile than she'd ever admit. 'I get shot *once*, and suddenly I'm work-shy?'

Nick was lounging in the visitor's chair with a punnet of grapes. 'Technically, your Kevlar took the worst of it. You've got a glorified scratch. Bit dramatic, really.'

'Oi, I'll give you a glorified scratch in a minute,' Kennedy quipped back.

Ruth laughed, the sound light and unexpected. She was enjoying the jokey atmosphere. It was the first time she'd let herself relax since the chaos in Bangor and Bala Lake. 'Honestly, you're lucky. Another inch and you'd have lost the use of your arm,' Ruth said with a more serious tone of voice.

'Shame. I could have been living the life of Riley, putting my feet up at home with my monthly injury benefits rolling in,' she joked. Then she frowned. 'I've been kept completely out of the loop since I arrived here. You need to bring me up to speed.'

Nick leaned forward, voice lowering just a fraction. 'We've ID'd Wolf. It was Sheila Clarke.'

Kennedy's eyebrows lifted. '*Sheila* Clarke? The stepmum?'

Ruth nodded. 'She's top of British Action. And she used poor Alfie as a pawn to manipulate Ray into withdrawing his statement. The whole thing was a smokescreen. She had to keep under the radar.'

Kennedy shook her head slowly. 'Jesus. That's cold. Even by far-right terrorist standards.'

'Still,' Nick said, tossing a grape into his mouth, 'you should've seen Ruth's face when she worked it out. She went full Poirot. All that was missing was the twirly moustache.'

Kennedy guffawed.

'Piss off,' Ruth rolled her eyes. 'You'll be walking home if you're not careful, Nicholas.'

There was a knock at the door and a cheerful nurse poked her head in. 'Doctor Williams says you're fit to leave here tomorrow, Jade. We just need to sort out some pain relief before you leave.'

'Thank you,' Kennedy said with a kind smile.

The nurse gave a thumbs-up and disappeared again.

'Right,' Ruth said firmly. 'You're taking the next week off. That's an order.'

'But...' Kennedy began.

'No buts,' Ruth interrupted. 'You've been shot.'

'The boss is right,' Nick said, uncharacteristically serious. 'Take your time and get some rest. Then come back and terrify us all with your efficiency.'

Kennedy sighed dramatically. 'Fine. A week. But only because I want to be in peak condition...' She paused. 'I've decided I'm putting in for the Sergeants' exams.'

Ruth smiled. 'Fantastic. You're sure?'

Kennedy nodded. 'Yeah. Your suggestion got me thinking. And I figured that if I'm going to be in a job where I get shot at, I might as well earn a few extra quid for the trouble.'

Nick snorted. 'You effectively want danger money, do you?'

'Exactly.'

Kennedy leaned back against the pillows, a crooked smile playing at her lips. 'Sergeant Kennedy,' she repeated softly, as if trying it on for size.

'Got a nice ring to it,' Ruth said.

Outside, the sun peaked from behind the cloud cover and shone against the glass window. And for the first time in days, it felt like things might just be all right.

CHAPTER 57

Inside Ruth's home everything was warm and quiet. The fire murmured in the hearth, casting long shadows across the wooden floor, while a stew bubbled gently on the stove in the kitchen.

Ruth sat curled at one end of the sofa, half-reading the news on her phone. Sarah was perched in the armchair opposite and sipped from a glass of wine.

Daniel lay stretched out on the rug, flicking through a dog-eared football annual. He'd barely spoken all afternoon, which was unusual.

Eventually, he broke the silence. 'Can I tell you guys something?'

Ruth lowered her phone. Sarah looked up too, her expression calm but expectant.

Daniel sat up, arms resting on his knees. His voice was quiet, but steady. 'I said sorry to those lads. The ones I punched. The ones that called you that word.'

Ruth blinked, putting down her phone. Sarah sat forward.

'You did?' Ruth asked gently.

He nodded. 'Yeah. At lunch break. I just... I went over and said I was sorry. For hitting them. I told them I still think what they said was wrong. But I shouldn't have reacted the way I did.'

Sarah smiled, just a little. 'That takes a lot of guts, Dan.'

He shrugged, fiddling with the corner of the rug. 'They were surprised, I think. But then they said sorry too. Said they didn't really mean it the way it came out. That they were just being stupid. Said they'd never met anyone with two mums before.'

Ruth watched him carefully. 'And how did that make you feel?'

Daniel gave a thoughtful shrug. 'Okay. I don't think they're bad lads. Just... a bit thick.' He cracked a smile. 'Anyway, we talked about the Wrexham match after that. I think we're all right now.'

Sarah leaned forward slightly, her voice warm. 'You did the right thing. That's how things change, you know. Not by punching, but by making people think.'

Daniel nodded, then lay back again on the rug, staring at the ceiling.

'You know what?' Ruth said after a pause, reaching down beside the sofa. 'I've got something for you.'

Daniel sat up again, curious.

Ruth pulled a Sports Direct bag from under the coffee table and handed it to him.

He opened it carefully, then gasped. 'No way!'

He pulled out the new goalkeeping gloves. Jet black with fluorescent green detail, thickly padded and pristine. His initials stitched across the wristband.

'These are the ones! The real ones!'

Ruth smiled. 'I thought you'd earned them.'

Daniel grinned and scrambled up, throwing his arms around her. 'Thank you, thank you, thank you.'

She hugged him tightly. 'You're welcome, sweetheart.'

Sarah looked over at them, eyes warm. The firelight flickered, the smell of stew wafted from the kitchen, and for a moment, everything was still.

CHAPTER 58

Nick closed Megan's bedroom door gently, taking a moment to listen for her breathing. It was soft, steady, safe. The nightlight cast a dim amber glow across the room, catching the corner of her unicorn poster and a few scattered picture books on the floor. He smiled faintly and stepped back onto the landing.

He paused by the window at the far end of the hall, peering out through the condensation-streaked glass. And there it was.

The car.

The same black Audi. The same spot across the road. Headlights off. Engine off and just sitting there in silence.

His chest tightened.

Not again.

Without thinking, Nick turned, his boots thudding down the stairs. The hallway felt longer in the dark. He yanked the front door open and stepped out into the chilly night.

The cold slapped him in the face, sharp and immediate.

The Audi driver's door clicked open.

Nick slowed, now cautious.

A man stepped out. He was tall, lean, hoodie drawn up, face half-hidden beneath the streetlight's glow.

Then Nick saw him clearly.

Shaun Keegan.

His pulse kicked in.

Nick braced himself. Was Keegan about to attack him?

But Keegan didn't move aggressively. He simply stood by the open door of the car, hands visible and calm.

'What the hell are you doing outside my house?' Nick growled as he strode forward. 'You think this is a game? I've got a wife and daughter in there.'

Keegan lifted his chin. 'I didn't want to come to your door. Not with your kid and missus inside.'

Nick stopped a few feet away, fists clenched, heart thudding in his ears. 'Then why are you here? Why the hell have you been watching me?'

Keegan exhaled, his breath visible in the cold. 'Because I needed to warn you.'

Nick blinked. 'Warn me? Warn me about what?'

Keegan stepped forward, lowering his hood. His face looked older now.

'They know, Nick. The Croxteth Boyz. They know what you did.'

A long silence opened between them. Only the groan of the wind.

Nick's breath caught. 'What are you talking about?'

'They know you had Curtis Blake killed. In prison,' Keegan said simply. 'They're not shouting about it. Not yet. But they've made a decision.'

Nick's stomach dropped hard. 'A decision?'

'They're going to kill you,' Keegan said. 'When the time's right. When your guard is down.'

Nick staggered back a half-step, not out of fear, but sheer disbelief. His mind raced.

'How do you know this?' he asked, his heart pounding.

Keegan's eyes flicked around, checking the shadows. 'Because I'm not who they think I am. Not who *you* think I am.'

Nick stared at him, narrowing his eyes. 'What the hell does that mean?'

Keegan took a breath. 'I'm undercover. Merseyside Police. Deep cover. I've been inside the Croxteth Boyz for five and a half years.'

The words hung there for a moment.

Nick shook his head slowly. 'No. That's bullshit.'

'I can prove it. But not now. Not here,' Keegan said quietly. 'I'm risking everything just talking to you. But you needed to know. They're patient. They'll wait for the right moment. That's when they'll strike.'

Nick's eyes burned into Keegan's. 'Why warn me? Why now?'

Keegan hesitated. 'Because you deserve to know.'

Nick let the silence stretch.

The man in front of him might be lying. Or telling the truth. And if he was telling the truth…

'What do I do?' Nick asked, voice low.

'Keep your wife and daughter safe. Vary your routes,' Keegan said. He turned, stepping back into the Audi. 'I'll be in touch when I can.'

The engine purred into life, headlights flooding the street. Then the car pulled away, taillights bleeding red into the darkness.

Nick stood alone in the cold.

He glanced up at Megan's window.

Then back at the empty street.

A shadow had passed over his life again. The ghost of Curtis Blake still haunting him.

CHAPTER 59

Kennedy sat upright on the hospital bed, the thin cotton blanket draped loosely across her legs. Her phone was already packed away, her bag zipped and ready. All she needed were the bloody painkillers and she could finally go home. The boredom was starting to get to her.

She glanced at the clock. Ten forty-seven a.m.

A soft knock on the door made her turn.

The hospital porter who stepped in wore light blue scrubs, a navy-blue baseball cap and a surgical mask stretched across his face. A laminated badge hung from a lanyard around his neck, and he pushed a wheelchair in front of him.

'Jade?' His voice was muffled by the mask, but calm. 'Time to head down to the dispensary. Once you've got your meds, you're a free woman,' he joked.

She looked at the chair, then back at him.

'I can walk,' she said. 'I don't need the wheels.'

He gave a small shrug. 'It's the ward policy. Especially post-op. Just makes life easier for all of us,' he said in a friendly, jovial tone. 'Anyway, it keeps an old bloke like me fit, pushing people around all day.'

Kennedy laughed. Her shoulder still ached, and she wasn't in the mood to argue over protocol. 'Oh, right. Well, if I'm basically doing you a favour...'

'You are,' he laughed.

As she lowered herself into the wheelchair, she nodded towards his mask. 'What's with the mask?'

He chuckled behind the fabric. 'Measles outbreak on the paediatric ward. We're all masking up again down there. Just being careful, you know.'

The explanation made sense. Sort of. She relaxed slightly as he wheeled her into the corridor.

They moved slowly down the ward.

Then the doors to the lift opened with a metallic clunk and they went inside.

As the doors slid closed, the man's grip on the handles tightened.

Kennedy frowned.

Something didn't feel right.

Then he leaned down slightly, his voice suddenly different. No trace of the cheery old man from a moment ago.

'It's been a while, DC Jade Kennedy.'

She froze. She recognised the voice. But from where?

The man reached up and peeled off his mask.

Ian Nesbitt.

Her stomach dropped.

'No.' She tried to get up, but his arm shot forward, fast, the glint of a needle catching the dull fluorescent light.

She felt the stab just below her jaw. It was sharp.

She tried to scream, but her limbs were already getting heavy.

Her vision blurred. Her heart punched against her ribs.

Nesbitt crouched in front of her as she slumped into the chair, breath shallow, muscles failing.

'Your pal, DS Nick Evans, had my lad killed,' Nesbitt sneered. 'Someone's got to pay for that. And you're the perfect fit. Black police officer? You're the crown jewel, Jade. They'll be talking about this for years.'

The lift hummed downwards.

Nesbitt pointed to the mirrored wall of the lift. 'I want you to remember how you look,' he whispered, brushing a strand of her hair aside. 'Because when they find you, you won't look like this, I can promise you that.'

The lift pinged.

The doors slid open.

And then everything went dark.

Your FREE book is waiting for you NOW

THE THEATRE STREET KILLING PREQUEL

South London 1995. A brutal murder.

Find out about Ruth Hunter and her move from Uniform to being a detective in CID.

Get your free prequel at

http://www.simonmccleave.com/vip-email-club

and join my VIP Email Club.

CANELOCRIME

Do you love crime fiction and are always on the lookout for brilliant authors?

Canelo Crime is home to some of the most exciting novels around. Thousands of readers are already enjoying our compulsive stories. Are you ready to find your new favourite writer?

Find out more and sign up to our newsletter at canelocrime.com